KILLING SUNDAY

Gina Amos

ISBN : 978-0-9923105-3-0

Kara Group Pty Limited
PO Box 277
Hunters Hill NSW 2110 Australia
ht@kara.com.au

First published 2014

Also By Gina Amos

Secrets and Lies

Killing Sunday is the second book in the series that follows the career of Detective Jill Brennan. Each book can be read on its own or as part of a series.

For the Italy Girls

But helpless pieces in the game. He plays,
Upon the chequer-board of Nights and Days
He hither and thither moves, and checks — and slays
Then one by one, back in the Closet lays.
The Rubáiyát of Omar Khayyám

Chapter One

The oars thud against the gunnels. With only fifty metres to the shore, he pulls back hard. Thunderous clouds pile on top of each other; they roll towards him like giant dragonheads. The light is fading fast; it's difficult to make sense of the dark shape. A dolphin caught in the netting? No, not this far up the river.

Broken waves slap against the dinghy. When he draws level with the Baths, he squints, tries to make sense of the shape. The black bag splits, the rope breaks free and trails away, the blubbery contents empty into the river. The wash caresses her gently and she rolls towards him. Tendrils of long, red hair drift about her shoulders like the tentacles of a giant sea anemone. Suspended, pale, weightless, the lower part of her body is submerged. What is left of her face is staring back at him, smiling.

Detective Inspector Nick Rimis opened the boot of his car. He struggled into the white polythene over-suit, hauled the hood into place and stuffed a face mask into his pocket. He walked down the ragged steps to the pale stretch of sand. It was a few minutes before seven in the evening. He had never been here before, didn't even know the place existed. It was an out-of-the-way Sydney suburb, at the end of a long peninsula; a dead end, leading nowhere; a place where the Parramatta and Lane Cove Rivers met. He flashed his ID at the female officer standing by the blue checkered tape and signed the log.

Apart from static chatter over the police radio, it was quiet, peaceful, a place where a group of professionals were getting on with the job. Scene of Crime Officers dressed in white hooded overalls and elasticised shoe covers shuffled around the boat sheds. Some were on their hands and knees sifting through the sand, while out on the timber boardwalk, another group had their heads down. Two divers in black wetsuits bobbed inside the netted enclosure.

Rimis stood outside the privacy tent with two male probationary officers at his side. Bruise-coloured clouds scuttled in from the east. A mortuary van had just arrived. He checked the time on his watch and wondered where Doctor Greer Ross was. Then, he saw her. She was dressed in a white SOC suit, just like everyone else, but somehow she managed to look stylish. The medical bag she was carrying was brand new. She nodded at Rimis. 'What have we got?' She pulled up her mask to cover her nose and mouth.

'See for yourself.' Rimis pulled back the tent flap and followed in behind her. The harsh glare of arc lights was trained on the bloated body. The mouth and jaw were loose and there was a hint of a smile. *Some joke.*

The young girl was unnaturally white, covered in Cutis Anserina, commonly known as gooseflesh. The right arm was missing. There was bruising and chafing on the left wrist.

'Do we know who she is?' Doctor Ross asked.

'We didn't find any ID on her. We're checking the MisPer register.'

There were voices outside the tent.

'The forensic photographer's here, boss,' one of the young officers called out.

The photographer walked around the body. He chose his shots carefully and with detachment. When he had finished, Doctor Ross knelt down and ran her white-gloved hands over the body. She gently pulled back the girl's hair and looked at what was left of the face. 'This is going be difficult. There are a lot of variables in a case like this.' Her attention shifted to the puffy thighs. 'Look at the puncture marks, intramuscular. Would have been painful.'

'An addict?' Rimis asked.

'Can't say.'

'Did she drown?'

'Can't say.'

'For fuck's sake woman, at least take a guess.'

Doctor Ross didn't look up. 'She's wearing joggers, so I don't think she went for a swim.'

Rimis pulled a face.

'Look, Inspector. I haven't got any quick answers for you. I'm not being difficult, it's just that I don't believe in guessing.'

Rimis loosened his tie. A crack of thunder boomed in the distance.

Doctor Ross looked over her shoulder at him. 'When a person drowns, the eyes glisten.'

Rimis moved closer to the body and looked into the young woman's eyes. Were they glistening? Well, they didn't look like it, but how would he know? 'How long do you think she's been in the river?'

'At least a week. A body usually floats after seven to ten days in warm water and the temp this time of year is around, what? Twenty-three, twenty-four degrees?' She didn't wait for him to answer. 'There's no sign of rigour. It's come and gone.' She tugged and removed one of the shoes. 'Take a look at the skin on the foot.'

The flesh peeled away like a sock. Rimis flinched, wiped his mouth with the back of his hand. If he could think of an excuse, he would leave now.

Doctor Ross moved her attention away from the foot and picked up the left hand. Rimis noticed the lacerations, the blue inky butterfly on the inside of the lower arm.

'What's the story with the missing arm?' Rimis looked at the skin on the stump. It was ragged; coils of muscle were hanging loose.

'Severed, not eaten.' Doctor Ross removed her mask and peeled back the hood of her SOC suit, letting her dark, wavy hair tumble over her shoulders. She picked up her medical bag. 'The trauma to the face could have happened at the same time.'

Rimis pushed back the vinyl tent flap. He ran his fingers through his dark, thick hair and walked to the water's edge. It was high tide so he didn't have far to go.

Tiny waves lapped at the shore. He had his back to the tent and drew in a long, deep breath to clear the stench from his lungs. The air smelled moist and salty. Christ, what he would do for a cigarette now. Times like these, he wished he had never given them up.

Doctor Ross snapped off her gloves and walked over to Rimis. The river was oily calm. The greyish blue sky, smeared with thin lines of mauve, had the look of a watercolour about it.

'Do you fish?' Rimis asked.

'Never tried. What about you?'

'Rather have them served up to me on a plate with chips.'

It was the first time Rimis had heard her laugh. Someone turned the floodlights on above the Baths and the place lit up like Christmas. The wind picked up. 'Looks like rain,' Rimis said.

'We should get her out of here. I'll be able to tell you more when I get her on the table.' She looked up at the gathering clouds and tightened the grip on her medical bag. She started to make her way back along the beach, stopped and turned around. 'Are you coming?'

'Have to finish up here first. I'll get there when I can.'

Rimis watched her go. The wind creaked through the Coral trees. He looked up at the access road which led down to the Baths and spotted the rows of curious locals, television crews, journalists and photographers. Bad news travels fast. A few people were holding their mobile phones in the air, taking photographs. Who knew? They might get lucky. Someone might capture something the police photographers had missed.

Two hours later, Rimis parked his car at the back of the morgue and made his way through the loading bay. He showed his ID to an attendant, signed the visitor's log, and walked down the long corridor to the security doors. They buzzed open. He pulled on a white lab coat, a mask, and a set of blue shoe covers and pushed his way through the swinging doors to the post mortem room. He stood on the threshold. An exhaust fan droned in the background, but it failed to block out the smells. His sensitive nose caught a whiff of formaldehyde, rotting flesh and antiseptic.

Doctor Ross was standing over the girl's naked body. She stopped what she was doing and turned to look at him. 'You took your time.'

Rimis smiled, but he didn't feel comfortable in this room; he never had. He walked up to the table, waited while she dictated into her machine.

A few minutes later, she turned it off. 'The search turn up anything?' she asked.

'Nothing. Looks like all we've got to work with is the garbage bag. There was nothing special about it,' he said.

Doctor Ross picked up a scalpel and removed the lungs from the chest. She placed them in a stainless steel kidney bowl. 'I thought as much.'

'What?' Rimis leaned forward.

'They're filled with fluid.' She picked up the soggy lungs and took a closer look.

'She drowned then?'

'Not necessarily.'

'What do you mean? Not necessarily?'

'Pulmonary foam. It can be caused by a number of things, including a drug overdose, but at this stage, I'm not ruling out death by drowning.' Doctor Ross turned to look at him. 'When someone drowns, they usually hold their breath and when they can't hold it any longer, they take a couple of short, desperate breaths and water is pumped into the lungs.'

'Fuck, Greer, tell me something I don't already know.' Rimis knew if Ashleigh Taylor were here, she would be more direct with him and wouldn't be treating him like some young probationary officer.

'No sign of sexual activity, if that helps. Overall, she was a healthy young woman.'

'Age?'

'Somewhere between eighteen and twenty judging by her dental eruptions. Third molars don't usually erupt until the early twenties. There's no evidence of them, so there's a clue.' Doctor Ross was taking a scraping of the tattoo. 'The jaw's intact and if we can get a hold of some dental records and take X-rays, it could be the easiest way to identify her. And the tattoo, it will help of course, unless it's recent.'

Without knowing who the girl was, Rimis knew the investigation was stalled. Thirteen names had come up on the MisPer register and not a butterfly tattoo amongst them. He shut his eyes and scrubbed his face with his hands. During his career, he had seen his fair share of corpses, but never enough to become used to them, especially when it came to women and children. 'I'll be at Otto's Bar if you haven't got anywhere better to go after you finish here.'

Rimis walked out into the night air and the nausea he had been feeling all evening began to fade.

Chapter Two

Fine weather usually brought the crowds, but Centennial Park was quiet for a Sunday morning. Rimis looked at his watch and turned to the crosswords on the back page of the newspaper. He would give her another five minutes and, if she didn't show by then, he'd head off to Otto's Bar for an early lunch.

'You're late.' He didn't look up.

'Sorry, boss.' Senior Constable Jill Brennan sat down next to him on the timber bench and left a polite gap between them.

He looked at her. 'What's that on your head?'

'It's a bucket hat.'

'It looks bloody ridiculous. You look like Inspector Gadget.'

'It does the job though, keeps the sun off my face. You know what the Cancer Council says, slip, slop, slap.' She smiled at him and crossed her legs.

He noticed a thin gold chain around her right ankle.

Silence.

Rimis knew from her personnel file, Senior Constable Jill Brennan was twenty-eight years old with a double degree in art history and law from Sydney

University. She was short, solidly built. She was also naturally beautiful. She wasn't wearing make up, not even lipstick. Her oval face was smooth, tanned. She was wearing white knee-length shorts, a pink singlet top and a pair of flat, strappy sandals. Rimis was jealous of her practical clothing and tried not to look at her bare legs. He'd been distracted by her more times than he wanted to admit.

He cleared his throat. 'So, what's been happening at the Gallery, then?

'Not much. I sent Freddie Winfred an invitation to Kevin's exhibition, but she didn't show. She could be out of town, or maybe she's got something better to do with her time.'

Jill Brennan had had a private school education. She should have had a private school voice, but she didn't. No airs or graces. Rimis put his newspaper aside. He saw her looking at the blank spaces of the cryptic crossword puzzle.

'Freddie Winfred is our only lead in this case and I want it off my desk. I've got more important things to worry about than art fraud.' Rimis tugged his collar, reached into his trouser pocket and pulled out a pack of mints. 'Want one?'

She shook her head.

'I heard about the girl at Woolwich Baths,' she said.

Rimis popped a mint into his mouth.

'Any leads?' she asked.

He turned and looked at her. 'You know what? You've got a long way to go before you become a detective. Just concentrate on the Winfred woman and leave the big cases to the big boys.'

Detective Inspector Rimis first met Brennan when they were investigating the Rose Phillips murder. He knew, even then, she was one of the most methodical and intelligent officers he had come across during his twenty-year career. Policing ran in her family. Her father, Detective Sergeant Mickey Brennan, had been killed in a drug raid in Lakemba four years ago. Six months later, she had thrown in her job at a high-end legal firm and joined the service.

Rimis knew she was determined to follow in her father's footsteps, but the road to becoming a detective wasn't always an easy one. It was still a male bastion, even in these days of equal opportunities. He was surprised when the Superintendent had asked him to keep an eye out for her. Whether it was out of respect for Mickey Brennan or her own abilities, he wasn't certain.

Rimis got to his feet and looked at the raft of Musk ducks on Busby's Pond. The mother duck dived below the surface to cool off. Her ducklings followed her lead. After they disappeared, he wriggled his toes inside his tight, laced Oxfords. He was tempted to remove them and soak his feet in the pond. 'I know it's not easy.'

'What do you mean?'

'Going undercover.'

'It's a one-off, and a low-risk assignment,' she said. 'We both know I wouldn't be sitting here if it wasn't for my degree in art history.'

Rimis knew she was right. The Special Forces Undercover Unit hadn't been able to supply an operative with any art knowledge or background. When a computer search of the personnel files came up with her name, she was the obvious choice.

'Christ, this has gotta be one of the hottest March days on record.' Rimis squinted at the sun and wiped the back of his neck with his hand. 'Should have told you to meet me out of the heat, somewhere with air con and cold beer on tap.' He put on his sunglasses, got to his feet and tugged at his trousers, damp with perspiration. 'Want you to know, if you play your cards right, you'll be working with me permanently after we wrap up this case. And then who knows? One day you just might make a half-decent detective.' Rimis picked up his newspaper, walked off towards his car and gave her a backhanded wave.

Later that afternoon, Rimis parked his car and walked down to the Sailing Club. He had gone home to change and was dressed in a pair of faded jeans, a checked navy and red shirt, and a baseball cap. He looked out at the river. It reminded him of the days he sailed sabots as a young boy on the Central Coast. He walked into the large open boat shed and looked at the empty racking and the walls, covered with marine charts, ropes and life buoys. It was a good day to be out sailing.

'Can I help you?'

'Yeah,' Rimis said. He pushed his sunglasses to the top of his head and flashed his warrant card. 'I'm Detective Inspector Nick Rimis from Chatswood Detectives. I wanted to ask you about the tides.'

'What do you want to know?' the old man asked.

'I suppose you know about the girl washed up at the Baths?'

'Yeah, it's usually pretty quite around here. When something like that happens, hard not for people to be talking about it. This is a family suburb, there's a strong sense of community here.'

Rimis knew he could have looked up the tide flows himself on the Bureau of Meteorology site, but he wanted to get a local's point of view. Anyway, he had nothing better to do with his Sunday afternoon.

'Your lot were here the other day, asking all sorts of questions. They were looking at the boats and wanted to know about the club members. They didn't ask about the tides.'

'I'm here now, and I'm asking,' Rimis said.

'Come with me, then.' They walked up a narrow set of swirling, orange-carpeted stairs to a small, dusty room. The old man sat down at a desk covered in marine charts, pushed them aside and logged onto the computer. Rimis leant into him and looked over the man's shoulder.

'Let's see now, she was in the water for what, a week you say.' He tapped the keyboard and checked the charts.

'That's right,' Rimis said.

He did a few calculations, sat back, and scratched his head. 'Chances are she would have come from over at Burns Bay. There's a boat ramp over there. The fishing's good in that part of the river. Do you fish, Inspector?'

Chapter Three

Jill walked through the doors of the New South Wales Art Gallery behind a group of cameramen. Whenever she came here, it was like she was seeing the gallery for the very first time. She crossed the patterned stone tiles in the foyer and looked up at the high ceilings. Usually conversations were hushed, but today she sensed the excitement and anticipation among the art fraternity who had come to witness the announcement of the Archibald Prize.

She made her way down two levels to the exhibition rooms, showed her invitation and was offered a glass of champagne and a catalogue.

The media was milling about the rooms, bumping into the crowd with their cameras and interviewing the artists. Jill was standing in front of the portrait of Father Bob Maguire when Kevin Taggart walked up behind her and tapped her on the shoulder. She turned around.

'I've been looking for you everywhere. I almost didn't recognise you in those clothes.'

Jill had taken extra care dressing this morning. She was wearing a blue, cowl-neck, silk tunic over a pair of white crop pants. A silver pendant hung around her neck. She had even applied some lipstick. She looked at Kevin's badly cut jacket and wondered why he didn't make more of an effort. It wasn't as if he couldn't afford to. 'You'll never guess who I've been talking to,' Jill said.

Kevin ignored her. 'Come with me,' he said and bounded off like an excited child.

They walked around the rim of the crowded room. Jill set down her empty glass on a passing waiter's tray and grabbed another champagne. 'I was talking to Ben Quilty, one of the finalists. Aren't you even a bit interested in what he had to say?' Jill had to run to keep up with Kevin. She pulled on his arm and spilled a few drops of champagne. 'For God's sake, Kevin, slow down.'

He ignored her and shouldered his way through a legion of journalists. 'There she is.'

'There's who?'

'Freddie Winfred, of course.' He scratched the back of his neck.

The crowd parted and Freddie Winfred's face broke into a smile. She walked up to Kevin and extended her hand. 'Zella Winfred, but call me Freddie, everybody does.' Folds of flame-pink silk billowed about her and hung on her ample body like washing pegged out to dry. 'I'm surprised our paths haven't crossed before today.' A smile travelled to her eyes, emphasising eyebrows plucked to within an inch of their life. '*North Coast Summers* deserved the Wynne last year. The way you captured the light. It was quite extraordinary.' Kevin opened his mouth to reply but Freddie was looking past him. She waved to someone in the crowd. She laughed. It was a sharp, raucous laugh. Kevin cringed. He looked down at the floor and studied his shoes.

Freddie turned back to him. 'Sorry I missed your exhibition. I've been out of town. I'll pop into The Dunworth later this week.' She finished what was left of her champagne in one mouthful.

'Everything's packed away in the stock room, except for *North Coast Summers*. The gallery's getting ready for the Byron Willis exhibition,' Kevin said.

Freddie turned her head and looked over her shoulder. 'Ah, there you are Dorin.' A well dressed man who appeared to be in his forties pushed his way through the crush, holding two glasses above his head.

Freddie took one of the glasses from him and grabbed him by the arm. 'Kevin, this is my dear friend and business associate, Dorin Chisca. He's from Romania.'

'Nice to meet you, Dorin.' Kevin shook his hand. 'So where's Romania?'

'It is on the Black Sea and borders Hungary,' Dorin Chisca said in a thick accent.

Jill cleared her throat.

'Sorry,' Kevin looked at Jill. 'I'd like you to meet Jill Brennan. She's a good friend of mine. She's also the assistant director at The Dunworth. For someone who's an ex-copper, she knows a hell of a lot about art.'

'You were a police officer? What an extraordinary career change, dear.' Freddie took both of Jill's hands in hers and held them tight. 'How on earth did you end up working at The Dunworth?'

'Belinda Travers. We grew up together. When I left the service, she offered me a position.' Jill looked down at the baubles on Freddie's fingers. They sparkled too much to be real.

'I know Bea,' Freddie said. Jill sensed she relaxed a little with the mention of her friend's name.

Kevin looked around him. 'Good crowd here today, Dorin. Seen anything you like?'

'These paintings are not to my taste.'

'What sort of art do you like then?'

'The Australian Heidelberg School, but you might know them as the Australian Impressionists.'

'Don't know much about them. I'm self-taught. Never had any formal training.'

'They painted in the plein-air in the impressionist tradition in the last part of the nineteenth century. They were inspired by the light and the Australian bush.'

An awkward pause.

'I have seen photos of your painting, *North Coast Summers.*'

'I painted it from memory. I spent a lot of time with my gran before she died. She lived on the Sapphire Coast, not far from Coffs Harbour.'

'It reminds me very much of my own family holidays. I spent time as a child in Constanta, a beautiful Romanian beach resort.' Chisca turned his attention to Jill. 'Excuse me, I hope you will not think me rude, but did you say you are a police officer?'

'Not any more. I'm working at The Dunworth Gallery now.'

'Ah, I see. And your last name? I did not catch it.'

'Brennan, Jill Brennan.' Jill took note of his neat hair cut, tailored dark suit.

'It is a pleasure to meet you, Jill Brennan.'

'So who do you think will win the Archibald this year, Mr Chisca?' Jill asked.

'I cannot say. This is my first time. Freddie tells me it is also called the *Archies*. I have noticed Australians like to shorten words. Perhaps it is because of your relaxed way of life.'

Jill laughed. 'You could well be right.'

'I am very surprised by all the excitement,' he said.

'Australians are very proud of the Archies.' Jill sipped her champagne and looked over the rim of her glass at him. 'You have to be a resident Australian artist to enter and the portraits have to be of a man or woman distinguished in arts, letters, science or politics.'

'And the Wynne and Sulman?'

'I can answer that,' Kevin said. 'The Wynne's awarded for the best landscape painting of Australian scenery, in either oils or watercolours, or for the best figure sculpture. The Sulman, for the best subject painting, genre painting or mural project. Only two artists have ever won the Wynne and the Archibald in the same year.'

'And who were they?' Chisca asked.

'William Dobell and Brett Whiteley. In 1978 Whiteley won all three awards. Can you believe it? The guy was a genius.'

Jill turned to Chisca. 'Do you know Brett Whiteley's work?'

Chisca didn't reply. The President of the Board of Trustees stepped up to the dais and flicked the microphone with his fingers. He cleared his throat and the room fell silent. The photographers and reporters stood ready to pounce.

It was just after six, when Jill parked her silver Golf around the corner from Bea and Harry Travers' neat, semi-detached house. The street was short and narrow, jammed packed with parked cars. Jill walked up the steps to the timber verandah and rang the doorbell. Harry opened the door and kissed her on both cheeks. 'Everyone's out the back,' he said. 'We were starting to think you weren't coming.'

'Sorry I'm late, the traffic was heavier than usual.' Jill handed Harry a bottle of wine and followed him down the hall to the back of the house.

'Hey, Bea, guess who I found on the doorstep?'

Bea threw her arms around Jill and stepped back to look at her. 'You look nice. How was the Archibald? I heard on the radio Tim Storrier won. I wish I'd gone with you, but with Callum sick, I didn't want to leave him.'

'Maybe we can go together one weekend. It runs for three months. Harry can mind Callum and we can make a day of it.'

'It's a deal,' Bea said.

Jill looked out to the backyard. A group of men were gathered around the barbecue. Women sat on chairs talking to each other, while toddlers crawled over them.

There were four couples. She hadn't met this group

of Bea and Harry's friends before. Young professionals with young babies. 'I feel a bit overdressed. Maybe I should have gone home to change.' Jill had driven straight from the Art Gallery and stopped only to pick up a bottle of wine from the local bottle shop.

'Relax. Have a glass of this.' Bea handed Jill a flute of French champagne then put the final touches to a tossed salad.

Bea and Jill had been friends since primary school and Jill wondered if her life could be anymore different from Bea's. 'So where's my gorgeous godson?'

'He's asleep, thank God.'

Get-togethers like these always made Jill feel uncomfortable. She didn't make friends easily. Alcohol helped, but she would have to watch what she drank tonight; she had to drive home.

Bea grabbed her by the arm and walked her outside. The temperature had dropped and with the cooler evening it was starting to feel more like autumn. Introductions were made. Bea's friends were a bit older than she was. They looked to be in their early to mid-thirties. Jill smiled, concentrated on names and made a fuss over their babies.

It was times like these Jill wished she had a partner. That way she might be able to disappear into the background and let someone else do the talking for her.

The doorbell rang. Bea jumped up but the conversation continued. Another guest had arrived. Bea set another place next to Jill.

'Sorry I'm late,' he said. 'Got caught up at work.'

'Everyone, this is Scott.'

The women stopped talking and looked at the latest

arrival. Their body language suddenly changed. They were smiling, adjusting their hair, and shifting in their seats. Scott walked over to join Harry at the barbecue.

Bea returned to the kitchen and a few minutes later the food was on the table. Everyone was now seated. Bea sat down across from Jill and passed her a bowl of salad. Jill looked Bea in the eye and gave her one of her ice queen stares.

'What?' Bea mouthed silently at her across the table.

This wasn't the first time Bea and Harry had tried to set her up with a blind date. She stole a look at Scott when he sat down beside her. He was certainly good-looking with a strong jaw, a tanned complexion and sparkling blue eyes. He had a boyish charm about him. Late thirties, early-forties she guessed, dressed well, spoke well, a professional. Probably worked with Harry. Harry was a gynaecologist. Jill was always joking with him that he got paid to do what most men would go to prison for.

Scott caught her looking at him and he smiled at her. Jill felt herself blush. At one stage his knee accidentally knocked against hers. He apologised and continued talking, taking centre stage.

The conversation shifted. The women were talking about babies, the men about cricket. Jill found herself in a conversation with Scott. He offered to fill her glass but she shook her head.

'So, how do you know Harry and Bea?' Jill asked.

'Harry and I play golf together when I can find the time. We met on the practice green. His handicap is better than mine, but I'm working on it.'

Jill told him she worked for Bea at her gallery and

found they shared an interest in art. She described the Archibald portraits she'd seen today, the ones she had liked and disliked.

Dessert came. The children were becoming restless; Callum had woken up and Harry was pacing around the backyard with him. The evening was winding down and it was only eight o'clock. Everyone apart from Jill and Scott prepared to leave. With children in tow, the couples walked back into the house. There was no delay in saying good-bye. They spilled out onto the footpath and drifted towards their cars.

Scott and Jill now found themselves alone. They both got up from the table. Jill cuddled Callum while Bea brought in the last of the plates and Scott helped Harry clean the barbecue.

Jill and Scott left together. 'Can I give you a lift somewhere?' she asked.

'I came by train. The station's only a few hundred meters.' They both looked down the street.

Jill turned back to him. 'Okay. Well, it was nice meeting you.'

'Likewise.' He brushed his lips against hers.

It was an awkward moment. After about twenty paces, Jill looked back over her shoulder and mumbled under her breath, 'Bea Travers, I'm going to kill you.' She knew Bea couldn't understand why she was still single. It wasn't that Jill didn't think it would be nice to have a man in her life, but she never felt as though she was missing out. Overall, she liked her life the way it was.

Her mother had died when she was only two years old and her father had never had a serious relationship in all the time she was growing up; at least, none she was aware of. It was only when she saw Bea and Harry together, that she realised she could be missing out on something special.

She drove back across the Harbour Bridge and realised she hadn't even asked Scott what he did for a living.

Chapter Four

Rimis had finished his caffeine hit for the morning and was hunched over his desk with a pen in his hand and a pile of reports in front of him. The girl washed up at Woolwich Baths still hadn't been identified. The enquiry had lost its initial momentum. New demands on time and manpower were being made.

They had been trying to put together an identikit picture of her but the face was barely recognisable. And he had hoped the tattoo would help, but Doctor Ross had told him it was recent. One of the team was checking tattoo studios across Sydney. He thought they might be able to locate the tattooist who carried out the work, but Jenny Choi had already told him most tattoo artists have their own distinctive style when it came to design or custom pieces. The artist would be recognisable by people in the know, but if the tattoo were picked off the wall in a tattoo shop, there wouldn't be a way to trace it back to the artist.

Off to one side of his desk, the Sydney Morning Herald was open at the cryptic crossword puzzle. He looked at the coffee rings and scribble smeared across the newsprint. He reached for his phone from under a pile of half-completed crime reports and dialled Brennan's number.

'This is Jill Brennan. I'm not available to take your call right now, so please leave a brief message.' Rimis hung up and tossed his phone in frustration across the desk. He thought about ringing the gallery's number, but less than a minute later his phone rang. He looked at the caller ID and expected it to be Brennan. He was surprised when it wasn't. It was Col Morrissey.

'Col, how did you go at Burns Bay?'

'We scoured the place, but it was *Clean up Australia Day* last Sunday. The Girl Guides did a good job. There were just a few McDonald's wrappers in the bushes they missed. We sent them off to Forensics, but I wouldn't hold your breath. You ever been there?'

'No.'

'Nice spot. There's a footy field, picnic tables, barbecues, and I was told it's good fishing in that part of the river.'

'Yeah, so I've heard.' Rimis said. 'You called me. So what have you got?'

'Thought you'd want to know. A DCI I worked with at the Federal Police phoned me. He retired a few years back after his wife died. You've probably heard of him, Ted Mackie?'

'Yeah, I remember Mackers, old school, good cop. I worked with him at Campbelltown for a while. How is he?'

'He's okay, but I thought you'd want to know.'

'Don't tell me he's organising a reunion or something?' Rimis flicked over a page of a report.

'No, nothing like that. It's Freddie Winfred.'

Rimis sat back in his chair. 'Freddie Winfred? What about her?' Rimis gave Morrissey his full attention.

'Hate to be the bearer of bad news, but it looks like she's missing.'

'What do you mean, missing? Missing on purpose, or missing, as in a missing person?'

'Hard to say. All I know is, her sister, Calida, seems to think something's happened to her. She reckons she wouldn't take off without telling her.'

'Well, I suppose she could be right. Middle-aged women don't usually disappear unless they've got a bloody good reason to. Tell me about Mackers. What's his connection in all of this?'

'He knows Freddie's sister. They both live at that fancy retirement village in the Hunter Valley. It's advertised on late night telly and in the Sunday papers. Acreage Hills. You heard of it?'

'No.' Rimis tapped his pen on the desk. 'So tell me, why does Freddie's sister think something's happened to her?'

'She hasn't returned any of her phone calls. Ted rang me to see what I could do after he'd checked all the hospitals and her neighbours. I didn't go through the usual channels because I know this art fraud case is sensitive.'

'You did the right thing. Leave it with me.' Rimis ended the call. Could Freddie Winfred have known they were onto her? Perhaps she developed a conscience or had become a threat to someone and needed to disappear for a while. Rimis tried Brennan's phone again and this time she answered after two rings. 'You at the gallery?'

'Hello boss, yeah I'm here. I was about to call you.'

'I thought I told you not to call me boss while you're undercover?'

'I keep forgetting. So, what do I call you then? Nick? Mr Rimis?'

'Don't be a smart arse. Call me, Nick.' Silence. 'Hope you've been studying for the Bull Ring.'

'Trying to.'

Rimis knew it could take years for her to get into the detective's education programme, if and when she passed the Bull Ring. He had no idea why the interview was called such a stupid name but remembered what it felt like as a twenty-five year-old constable to sit in front of three detective inspectors and answer four questions from fifteen broad topics. He had studied every piece of legislation and standard operating procedure available to him. It was still the most stressful experience of his career.

'So,' Rimis said, 'what are you doing besides dusting the pictures?'

'Paintings.'

'Yeah, okay then, paintings.'

'I've phoned Freddie's gallery a couple of times, but all I get is her answering machine. Thought I'd ring first before fronting up.'

'You might be waiting a while,' Rimis said.

'What do you mean?'

'She's missing. Her sister reckons something has happened to her.'

'You're kidding me.'

'No, I don't kid. First up, I want you to go to her gallery, see what you can find out. Then I want you to check her apartment, talk to the neighbours, see if they know anything, and Brennan —'

'Yeah, Nick?'

'Tell me you've got her address.'

'Of course I have, give me some credit. Why are you giving me such a hard time?'

'You don't have any training in undercover; you're not even a detective. What are you doing there at that gallery anyway?'

'It all takes time. I'm trying to establish myself. I've contacted all the gallery owners in the area. It's not as if I volunteered for this assignment.'

'Okay, I'm sorry.'

'No, you're not.'

Rimis leaned on his elbow. 'Look Brennan, I'm not going to have a slinging match with you. If I say I'm sorry, I'm sorry. Okay? I'm under a lot of pressure from the Super. For both our sakes, we need to solve this case.' Rimis rubbed the back of his neck and sat back in his chair.

Silence.

'You still there?'

'Yeah, I'm still here,' she said.

'Look, there's something else I want you to do for me.'

'What is it?'

'I want you to keep an eye on Taggart. I want you to keep him close, let me know what he's up to.'

'Kevin?'

'He's an artist isn't he? He could be mixed up in this art fraud business and I wouldn't be surprised if he has something do with Freddie Winfred's disappearance. I know I don't have to remind you he was a suspect in Rose Phillips' murder.'

'Kevin had nothing to do with that.'

'I was thinking more about his other neighbours, Edi and Rhoda Blake.'

'I might be out of line here, but I thought we were investigating art fraud.'

'We are, but I want another crack at Taggart. The Blake deaths were more than an accident.'

Jill knew about Rimis's obsession with Kevin Taggart and the Blake sisters. He had taken the case personally and she wondered why. 'But the Coroner said —'

'I don't give a monkey's what the Coroner said.'

The next phone call Rimis made was to the Acreage Hills Retirement Village. He left a message for Ted Mackie to phone him.

Chapter Five

A line of sweat trickled down Jill's spine. The sun was high and hot and the forecast was for another thirty-degree day, the third in a row. A hot westerly wind had just hit, bringing with it clouds of fine dust. She stepped off the footpath and crossed the road to the Winfred Gallery. She walked up to the front door and pressed the brass bell and peered through the shop front. She pressed it again. There was no movement or sign of life.

She remembered there was a car park off the rear entrance and walked around the corner. The car park was empty, apart from a red van. From the case notes, Jill knew Freddie drove a red Berlingo. She cupped her hands against the rear window and looked inside. A large calico drop sheet was rolled up into a ball.

There was no answer when she knocked on the back door of the gallery. She pulled out a pair of disposable gloves from the pocket of her jeans and tried the door handle. She was surprised to find it unlocked. There was no sign of forced entry.

'Hello? Anybody here?' Halfway down the hall she found an office. The door was wide open and in the middle of the room sat a Regency desk; behind it, a red leather padded chair. The desk was littered with art catalogues, a half-empty coffee cup and a pile of invitations for an exhibition at the gallery in less than two weeks time.

She pressed the play button on the answering machine and counted ten messages from someone she assumed to be Freddie's sister. The first message hinted at irritation, the last echoed concern. She heard her own messages and a number of general enquires. Most of them related to the gallery's opening hours and the upcoming exhibition.

Freddie's mobile phone was on the desk next to a phone charger. The phone was out of battery. Strange. Why would Freddie leave her phone behind? Jill removed the SIM card and tucked it into the hip pocket of her jeans. The service provider would be able to give her a list of recent calls. She hoped Freddie had the sense to save her contacts to the card.

Jill sat down behind the desk and looked around Freddie's office. If she found any evidence, it would be inadmissible in a Court of Law but she reminded herself she had entered through an open door.

She tipped the contents of the waste paper bin onto the floor and picked up a crumpled scrap of yellow paper. '*I know what you're both up to and it's going to cost.*'

Jill realised if Freddie knew someone was onto her, it made sense for her to disappear. Jill scanned the crumpled note with her phone and returned it with the rest of the debris to the bin. She looked around for anything she might have missed before walking into the exhibition room.

The paintings on the white plaster walls were impressive; watercolours, landscapes and portraits. One painting in particular caught her eye. It was a Dickerson. She had seen it before, but she couldn't remember if it was in one of her art books or at a gallery. There was something about it that didn't look right to her. She walked up to it and ran her gloved fingers over it. She was certain it was a fake.

Jill walked back out into the heat and the dust and pulled the gallery door closed behind her. She couldn't shake off the feeling something had happened here. She phoned Rimis to tell him about the note and the mobile phone left behind, but his number was busy. She left a message for him to call her.

She walked around the side of the building. A small midden of soggy cigarette butts was on the ground next to her feet. She didn't know if Freddie was a smoker, there had been no sign of cigarettes or an ashtray in her office. She pulled out a plastic zip-lock bag and scooped them up.

'Are you looking for Freddie?' A woman's voice called out from across the fence.

Jill stuffed the plastic bag into her shoulder bag and spun around. 'I am. I'm meant to be meeting her here to pick up a painting.' Jill walked over to her.

'Kat,' said the woman. 'I won't shake your hand. I've had them in the compost bin. Can't talk long either, I only came out here to get rid of some stems.' Kat looked to be in her early forties. She had bleached-blonde hair and a nose piercing.

'I was looking for Freddie. I don't suppose you've seen her?' Jill asked.

'Not for over a week. But that's not unusual. She's always gadding about the place, going off to some exhibition or other, or else going up to the Hunter Valley to visit her sister.' She looked over at the Berlingo. 'That's strange. Her van's still here.'

Jill turned around. 'Has it been here all week?'

'I'm not sure. I always use the front entrance to the shop but it's not like her to leave it here and go off somewhere. She hates public transport.'

'When did you say you last saw her?'

'Sunday. It was morning, early. I remember because I was out the front talking to a customer about the hydrangeas. I'd popped a few bunches in the buckets and he wanted to know how to change the colour from blue to pink. A car pulled up. I waved, but Freddie didn't see me.'

'What sort of car was it?'

'It was black. I think it was a Bentley, but I can't be sure. Just about everyone around here drives expensive cars. It's hard to tell one from the other.'

'Did you see the driver?'

'Yeah, he got out of the car, but he didn't open the door for her. Just goes to show, doesn't it? Just because you've got money, doesn't mean you've got manners. There was someone in the back seat. She climbed in there with them.' Kat wiped her forehead with the back of her hand and looked at Jill. 'I didn't like the look of him.'

'The driver or the passenger?'

'The driver. I didn't see the passenger. He was short, angry looking. He had a black leather jacket on. Too hot for leather, I thought. Why are you asking all these questions? You don't think something's happened to Freddie, do you?' Jill noticed Kat looking at Freddie's van again.

'I don't think there's anything to worry about. She's probably gone on a holiday, forgotten about our arrangement.' Jill had to remind herself she was the assistant director of The Dunworth Gallery. She wasn't a police officer now. She had to stop acting like one.

'Here's my card. Can you call me if you see her?'

'Sure.' Kat ran her hands down her shirt before she took the card. Jill noticed the woman's rough hands and the dirt under the stunted nails. Kat looked at the card.

'You're the Assistant Director at The Dunworth? With all the art galleries around here, I'd be out of business if there were as many florists. Freddie reckons yours is one of the better ones though.'

'That's good to know.'

Jill tried ringing Rimis again, but there was still no answer on either his direct line or his mobile phone. It was already eleven-thirty. She had arranged to meet a client at the gallery at midday and Bea was coming in at three to go through the accounts and to talk about some ideas she had for the Willis exhibition. Jill decided to pay a visit to Freddie's apartment in Darlinghurst during her lunch break.

Rimis drove north along the Pacific Highway, through the leafy suburbs of Killara and Turramurra. The traffic was moving at a steady pace. The air con was set at a comfortable twenty-two degrees. He turned right onto the motorway and put his foot down. He pressed the button on the CD player and sang along to his favourite Lisa Ono CD. *The Girl from Ipanema* was playing. He wasn't a good singer; he was off-key for most of the time, but his Portuguese was perfect (the lyrics were the only Portuguese he knew).

He stopped singing when he came up behind a car travelling below the speed limit. He flashed his lights. The car drifted to the inside lane where it should have been. Rimis grabbed the wheel tight and overtook him. 'Bloody idiot, hand in your licence and do everyone a favour.' Times like this, he wished he were still working the highway patrol between Calga and Morrisset.

He took a deep breath and knew there was no need to rush. Calida Winfred wasn't going anywhere. He started singing again and looked out at the road ahead.

Forty-five minutes later, he left the motorway. He passed a tractor. It was harvest time and the roads in and around the Pokolbin vineyards were clogged with farm machinery and bins. He looked out across the rolling countryside to the acres of woody vines and thought about the bottles of fine Hunter Shiraz they would produce.

After a few wrong turns, he saw the sign to Acreage Hills, took a hard right, drove down a narrow gravel road and followed a sandstone block wall for almost fifty metres until he came to the entrance. *Acreage*

Hills Vineyard, A Seniors Country Living Experience was etched on a polished brass plaque.

He had read up on Acreage Hills before setting out. The place was a boutique retirement village, set amongst the grape vines, an hour and a half's drive from the outskirts of Sydney. It was designed as a luxury country retreat by a leading firm of Sydney architects. There were twenty cottages located on an artificial lake and assisted-care for forty residents in the main building.

The main building had two wings. An arts and crafts room, a library, and card room were in the east wing. The west wing was the accommodation wing. It was also where the dining room and the communal lounge rooms were located. The village boasted a well-equipped gym, a croquet lawn and a twenty-five metre pool. Medical staff was on duty twenty-four hours a day.

Rimis entered through the iron gates. He passed a small plot of vines and noticed the roses at the end of each row. With the well-maintained lawns and large, stone urns filled with white flowers, he felt like he was entering a prestigious country club and wondered what it would be like to live in a place like this.

He drove into the gravel car park and took his pick of the empty spaces. He got out of his car, walked past the Jacaranda trees, and followed a red arrow pointing towards reception.

'I'm Detective Inspector Rimis from Chatswood Detectives,' he said to the woman behind the desk. He mopped the sweat from his forehead with a crumpled brown handkerchief. 'I'm here to see Ted Mackie. Any idea where he might be?'

'I'm Jasmine.' The woman pointed to the nametag on her chest. Her eyes brightened. From her reaction, Rimis imagined it had been a while since she had dealt with anyone under fifty-five. She didn't seem to mind that he could do with a closer shave or a new suit.

'He's sitting with Calida Winfred, over there under the tree next to the croquet lawn.'

Rimis's eyes shifted away from her exposed cleavage to where she was pointing.

'I can take you to him if you like,' she said.

'I can manage,' Rimis smiled and walked out the way he had come. He stepped off the timber verandah and into the blazing sunshine. There was no hint of a breeze, only the hum of cicadas. He recognised Ted Mackie from his shock of grey hair and the set of his broad shoulders. He walked up to him and felt the strength in Ted's hand.

'Nick, it's been a few years.' Ted Mackie was dressed in a pair of faded cargo shorts and an orange Hawaiian shirt dotted with pineapples. *Aloha* was printed above his shirt pocket in thick white letters. The country life seemed to agree with him and Rimis hoped that, when he was in his sixties, he would look as good as Ted Mackie did.

'Love the shirt,' Rimis said.

'Brought back a suitcase full of them. Cheap as chips.'

Rimis couldn't think of anything more to say; different times, different ranks, different jokes now. He tried to call on the names of colleagues they may have known, but his memory failed him. He looked across at Calida Winfred.

'You still married to that Detective Constable?' asked Ted. 'What was her name?

'Fiona,' Rimis said.

'That's right, Fiona. She was a good officer. Smart and a good looker, to boot. Great combination in anyone's books.'

'She left me a couple of years ago.' Rimis realised it still hurt to talk about his ex-wife, but she had obviously left her mark on Ted Mackie. It was hardly surprising. Fiona was one of those women who attracted men's attention without knowing it.

'I'm sorry to hear that.'

Rimis noticed the embarrassed look on Ted's face and shifted his attention to the woman standing beside him.

'I'm forgetting my manners,' Ted said. 'This is Calida Winfred. Cal, this is Detective Inspector Rimis.'

Rimis held out his hand. He was surprised by how steady and strong her handshake was. He sat down next to her and looked across at the wheelchair parked a few metres away. A brightly coloured crocheted rug was thrown across the seat and he wondered why she needed it.

'Miss Winfred, Ted tells me you think something's happened to your sister.'

'Yes, I'm sure of it. I'm worried about Freddie, Inspector, really worried. And please, call me, Cal.' She fanned herself with a folding paper fan.

'All right then.' Rimis took his notebook out from

the inside pocket of his jacket. 'So, when did you last speak to Freddie?'

'I remember exactly when it was. Last Monday. She was running late because she had been to the Archibald. She goes every year. She was hot and flustered when she arrived and stayed only long enough for a cup of tea, a biscuit, and to take a look at my innuendos.'

'Innuendos?'

'An inference to another artist's work.'

'You mean a fake.'

'Well, I suppose you could call them that, but I don't like the word. It sounds a little coarse.'

Rimis wondered if Calida Winfred was as naive as she appeared. Did she really expect him to believe she had no idea what her sister was up to? And Ted Mackie, couldn't he see what was going on here, or was he too besotted with the woman not to realise? Rimis looked at Ted, then back again to Calida.

'So, what does Freddie do with these innuendos of yours?' Rimis removed his jacket and loosened his tie.

'She sells most of them to investors. There's quite a market with the high cost of insurance these days. The originals are usually locked away in a bank vault while the innuendos are hung in homes or offices.'

'I see,' Rimis said. 'And how much does Freddie pay you for your pictures?'

'Paintings, Inspector, they're paintings.'

'Of course. So, how much does Freddie pay you for your paintings?'

'She covers the cost of materials and a little extra, but it's not about the money. I'm just happy to be painting again and to know my work's appreciated.' She stopped fanning herself and looked at Rimis. 'There's nothing illegal about them, you know Inspector, if that's what you're thinking. They weren't being passed off as originals. There's a difference, you know.'

'I know the legality of what you've been doing, Cal.' Rimis said. He looked at her and remembered why he was here. 'Ted tells me Freddie hasn't returned your phone calls. Maybe she's busy with other things and hasn't had the time to call you.'

'Freddie either rings me or I ring her every other day. It's a habit we've got into over the years, especially as we've grown older.' Calida pulled out a lace-edged handkerchief from her skirt pocket and wiped her nose. 'We've only got each other.'

'How did she seem when you last saw her? How was her state of mind?'

'She was preoccupied, now that I think about it.'

'Did she say why she was so keen to see you?'

'She wanted to take a look at my latest paintings. She was pleased with the last lot and took most of them away with her. She wanted me to try my hand at some Whiteleys. She knows I don't like his work, but she wouldn't take no for an answer. Before she left, she told me she would be back for them last Saturday.'

'And did you paint the Whiteleys?'

'Yes, and they're very good, even if I do say so myself. It would be hard to pick between them and the originals, unless you were an expert. I left a message on her machine to tell her I'd painted them, but when she didn't return my calls or show up here on

Saturday, I began to worry. That's when I spoke to Ted. I knew he would know what to do.'

Rimis looked at Ted Mackie. 'I'm sure there's nothing to worry about. She's bound to turn up. Don't you think, Ted?'

Calida looked at the two men. 'How can you be so sure?' The tears came. 'I know something's happened to her. I can just feel it.'

'I've checked all the hospitals,' Ted said, 'and the emergency departments, in case she had an accident. I even phoned her neighbour, but she hadn't seen or heard from her.'

'It does sound a bit odd, but in a case like this there's usually a reasonable explanation.' Rimis looked towards the cottages by the artificial lake. 'Mind if I take a look at your paintings?'

'I'm not in the cottages; I have a room in the main building. A year ago there was a terrible accident – a house fire and my legs were badly burned. I moved up here to get away from Sydney. That was when Freddie took over the running of the gallery.' Calida held the fan close to her chest. 'I lost everything in that fire.'

'Listen Cal, how about we walk back inside? We'll leave the chair behind,' Ted said.

'Perhaps I should.' Calida looked across at her wheelchair. 'We both know I don't need it. Freddie used to say I was only hanging onto it because I was looking for sympathy.'

Rimis looked at Ted and Calida and wondered about their relationship. Was it friendship or something more?

It was mid-afternoon when Rimis turned off the M1 and headed back along the Pacific Highway towards Chatswood. Progress through the traffic was slow, enforced by the forty kilometres per hour school zones and speed cameras.

Rimis's mind went back to Calida Winfred's room; to the colourful flowers in a vase, the trinkets on the window sill, a faded photo of two girls. The room resembled an art auction house and was filled with canvases stacked against the walls, three deep in some places. The Whiteley nudes in the walk-in robe. A punter like him wouldn't be able to tell the difference between a copy and the real thing. He wondered what Brennan would make of them and if they were as good as Calida Winfred seemed to think.

Chapter Six

Jill walked into Otto's Bar.

'Brennan, over here.' Detective Sergeant Morrissey didn't stand, but watched her as she made her way towards him. She sat down at the rocky table and placed her foot on the base to steady it.

'Name your poison,' he said.

'Soda with lemon.'

He gave her a look.

Jill rolled her eyes. 'Yeah, I know. I'm on this detox thing, giving the liver a rest for a while,' she lied. Jill knew alcohol was out of the question tonight because she needed a clear head to process whatever Morrissey was going to tell her.

Morrissey walked over to the bar and ordered. He returned to the table with a fresh beer and placed her drink in front of her. 'Here you go, one soda with lemon.' Morrissey swallowed a gulp of beer. 'So, how's the art fraud case going?'

'Not too good now the prime suspect is missing.' Jill took a sip of soda and changed the subject; she wasn't here to talk about Freddie Winfred. 'Thanks for agreeing to talk to me.' She couldn't summon the words, *about my father's murder.* After four years, she had finally read the case notes. She had never wanted to know the details before – it had always been too painful, too raw. She now realised she needed to know the facts if she was ever going to move on with her life.

Morrissey was with her father the night he was gunned down. When she was transferred to Chatswood LAC, she was surprised when she found out Morrissey was also stationed there. She had been waiting for the right moment to speak to him privately. She wanted to know first-hand what he could remember about that night.

'Look, Brennan, I don't know what you want me to tell you. It's been a long time.'

Too Long.

'I pulled the file from Archives. I've read the reports, looked at the photos and the forensics. I read your statement, but I don't understand why Dad forced his way into the house. There's no one else I can ask. Bill Peruzzi resigned six months ago. Did you know he died a few weeks ago? Liver cancer.'

'Yeah, I heard about Blinky,' Morrissey said.

'Blinky?'

'Yeah, as in Blinky Bill. Rotten business the big C. Blinky was a good bloke.' Morrissey took a slug of beer.

'You said in your statement you thought Chisca was in the house that night.'

'Did I?'

'Yeah, you did.'

'Well, if that's what my statement says, then I suppose you're right. Look Brennan, it was four years ago. A lot's happened since then. The world's moved on and maybe you should too. Just leave it alone. You're supposed to be undercover. You shouldn't even be talking to me. My advice is concentrate on finding Freddie Winfred instead of worrying about what happened to Mickey.'

'Why are you fobbing me off?'

'I'm not fobbing you off. Mickey took an unnecessary risk that night. It was supposed to be a simple surveillance operation. I don't know what got into him. He just went fucking crazy.' Morrissey looked at his watch.

'You got somewhere to go?'

'Yeah, it's my mum's birthday. We've booked a table at a restaurant in Parramatta.'

'You're lucky you've got a mum,' Jill said. 'Mine died when I was a baby, never knew her. Dad brought me up. He was my family.'

Morrissey raised an eyebrow. 'Tough call. Car accident wasn't it?'

'Yeah.' Jill looked down at her drink.

Morrissey nodded and ran his fingers through his hair. 'Listen, I liked Mickey, I really did. But I didn't know him that well. I met him at Redfern after I transferred from the AFP.' Morrissey leaned into the table, finished his beer. 'Look, I don't want you to get caught up in something that could affect your career.'

'What do you mean?' She was looking at him now.

Morrissey lowered his voice. 'Mickey was in over his head in debt. He had all sorts of loans and they weren't with financial institutions, if you catch my drift.'

'Dad corrupt?' She crossed her arms and sat back in her chair and looked at him. 'I don't believe you.'

Morrissey pushed his glass across the table. 'How much money did he leave you?'

'None of your business,' she said.

'My advice is to forget we ever had this conversation.' Morrissey picked up his car keys and pushed his chair back from the table. 'A word of advice.'

Jill looked at him.

'Let it go,' he said.

Chapter Seven

Jill put aside her coffee and was about to give Bea a call when she heard the Gallery's front door open. She got up from her desk.

'This is a surprise. What are you doing here?' She smiled at William Phillips and realised she was glad to see him.

'Thought I'd come and take another look at Kevin's exhibition, but it looks like I'm too late.' He looked at the empty walls.

'The exhibition finished last Friday. We're waiting on a shipment of Byron Willis's paintings. If you're interested, I can send you an invitation.'

'I'd like that. Got time for a coffee?'

Jill looked at her watch. 'A quick one.'

They walked across the road to the coffee shop and sat down at a table by the front door. From where they sat, Jill could see if anyone entered the gallery. They ordered coffee, a cappuccino for her and a double espresso for him.

'I have a confession to make.' William looked into her eyes and gently stroked the back of her hand. 'I didn't come to the gallery to see Kevin's exhibition. I came to see you.'

Jill looked down at his hand on hers. After his mother's murder investigation had ended, Jill hadn't heard from him again. At the time, she thought it was because she wasn't an easy person to get to know. She was also a police officer. She had the feeling her choice of career didn't sit easily with him.

'I don't know what to say,' Jill said. William was old enough to be her father and was carrying enough baggage to fill an Airbus A-330. She had problems of her own: there were questions about her father's death she needed answers to, especially now that Morrissey was alleging he was corrupt; the prime suspect in her undercover operation was missing; and she still had to sit the Bull Ring.

'You don't have to say anything, just come to dinner with me.'

Jill took back her hand and tucked her hair behind her ear. She knew William liked opera, ballet, and expensive dinners. She liked the beach, Thai food, and cheap wine. She skimmed a scoop of milk froth with a spoon.

'Apart from wanting to see you, I also wanted to ask your advice,' William said.

Jill raised her eyebrows. She crossed her legs and looked at him. 'What sort of advice?'

'I wanted to ask you about some paintings Stockland and Lewis bought.'

'What do you want to know?' She swallowed a spoonful of froth.

'You remember the Miró in my office?'

'Of course I do. How could I forget it? Don't get me talking about Joan Miró, William, or we'll be here all day.'

'I think it could be a fake,' he said.

Jill put down her spoon and looked up from her coffee.

'Our accounts people have been going through the assets register. We're missing provenance certificates. Can you tell by looking at a painting, if it's the real thing? If the Miró turns out to be a fake, there's a very good chance the rest of the art works on our office walls are fakes as well.'

She remembered the day she walked into his office and broke the news to him that his mother had been found dead in the kitchen of her house. That was when she had noticed the Miró on the wall behind his desk. There had been no doubt in her mind, even then, that it was anything but an original.

'I'm no expert when it comes to authenticating original art. It's a specialist field. Maybe if you contact the gallery where you bought it, they might be able to help.'

'I'd like you to have a look at it before I call them. Have you got time to come by my office and tell me what you think?'

'I can probably get away on Wednesday, during my lunch break.'

'Perfect.' William sat back in his chair. 'It makes you wonder why anyone would buy a major work of art with all this talk of art fraud in the papers. It must be affecting business at The Dunworth.'

'The Gallery has a good reputation and we always issue a certificate of authenticity. But, to be honest, even they aren't worth the paper they're written on.' Jill finished her coffee. 'What was the name of the gallery where Stockland and Lewis bought the paintings?'

'It was The Winfred. They're supposed to be reputable dealers.'

Chapter Eight

The hotel where Kevin Taggart had arranged to meet Dorin Chisca dated back to the fifties and smelt of stale yeast and fried food. It was an ugly, red brick building, located on a corner. A chalkboard out the front advertised two steaks for the price of one on Tuesday nights.

Kevin sat on a barstool. He had one foot on the timber rung, the other on the floor. He gulped down a mouthful of beer and raised his eyes to the wide, flat screen television above the bar. Australia was playing Sri Lanka at the Adelaide Oval. The Australians were batting and there was an occasional roar from the crowd when a batsman scored a run.

The early lunchtime crowd looked like they had been here since breakfast – pokie-playing pensioners, most of them.

'You reckon Sri Lanka's gonna win this match?' one of the drinkers called out.

Kevin turned around to face him. 'Not a bloody chance, mate.'

Dorin Chisca was fifteen minutes late according to the clock on the far wall. Kevin was hungry. He'd overslept this morning and had missed his breakfast.

He studied the blackboard menu and tried to decide between the nachos or the steak sandwich with fat chips.

'What'll it be today then, lovey?'

'Hello, Sheryl.'

The barmaid's fleshy mouth twitched. 'The Thai fish cakes are nice if you can't make up your mind.'

Kevin leaned forward on the stool and drummed the bar with his knuckles. 'Make it the usual. I can't go past your steak sandwich.' Sheryl mumbled something under her breath on her way back to the kitchen.

'Mr Taggart?'

Kevin spun around. The man placed his hand on his shoulder. 'Don't get up, no need. My name is Nicolae Vladu. I am associate of Mr Chisca. He has asked me to meet you because he has other business.'

The bartender walked up to them. 'What can I get you, mate?' He wiped the bar without making eye contact.

Vladu ordered an orange juice.

Kevin pointed to the blackboard. 'They do a great steak sandwich and chips if you're hungry.'

'It is too early to eat.' Vladu looked around the bar. 'This place is good. I can see everyone is minding their business.'

'How long you been in Australia then, Nicolae?' Kevin swallowed the last of his beer and put his glass on the counter cloth.

'We are not here to socialise. We have business to discuss.'

Kevin cleared his throat. 'Well, down to business it is. So, then, Mr Chisca wants to buy *North Coast Summers,* does he?'

'Yes and here is what you will do. Tell the Dunworth Gallery you wish to withdraw the painting from sale. Mr Chisca will pay you good price, cash, without middleman. Everyone will be winners.'

'Winners. I like the sound of that.' Kevin rubbed his hands together and thought of the hefty commission he would save by not selling his painting through the Dunworth.

Kevin's meal arrived. He walked to the end of the bar and picked up a large plastic tomato sauce bottle from a long table. He returned to his bar stool and oozed the thick sauce over the chips. 'I'll speak to them at the gallery. I'll make up some excuse.' He licked up a drip of sauce from the side of his hand.

'Good, it is agreed then. Mr Chisca has a warehouse in Chatswood. I will meet you there when you have the painting.' Nicolae looked over at the remainder of Kevin's meal and winced.

'And the other matter?' Kevin wiped his mouth with the back of his hand.

Vladu reached into the inside pocket of his leather jacket and pulled out a small package. 'With Mr Chisca's compliments, a sign of good faith, you understand.'

Kevin took the package and tucked it into his trouser pocket. He was trying to think up a suitable biblical quotation, but there wasn't much reference to drugs in the bible.

'Sure you wouldn't like a chip, Nicolae?'

Vladu looked at the spot of tomato sauce on Kevin's chin and left.

Jill hadn't slept well; she had tossed and turned most of the night. Col Morrissey's revelation about her father had shocked her. She thought back to when her father was still alive. There was nothing about his behaviour that had been odd or surprising but she realised it was unlikely she would have known if anything had been troubling him. Mickey Brennan never discussed his work with her, except if something amusing had happened at the station, or if there was a moral lesson to be learnt from one of the cases he was working on.

She tapped her computer keyboard and checked her emails. She was expecting the shipment of Byron Willis paintings to arrive early this morning but the transport company had phoned to say they were running behind schedule. Their van wouldn't arrive until around eleven-thirty. Bea had given her a list of names for the invitations and she still had to go through and check the addresses.

Before starting on the list, Jill removed the SIM card from her phone and replaced it with the card she'd found in Freddie's office. She entered the names from Freddie's contact list onto a spreadsheet. After almost five minutes of typing, she came across a name she recognised. *Kevin Taggart.* She bit down on her lip. With Freddie missing, she wondered if Rimis was right about him, but she dismissed the idea. Kevin Taggart a murderer? Ridiculous.

She ran her eye down the list. There was Calida, her sister, listed under C, Dorin Chisca, under D, and the usual personal services – her hairdresser, dentist, doctor. Peter Watkins was there under W. She remembered meeting him at the *Archibald*. He was the director of a gallery in Mosman and they had talked for some time about post-impressionism techniques. None of the other names meant anything to her.

The removalist van finally arrived and she took delivery of the paintings without incident. She grabbed a bottle of spring water from the kitchen fridge and typed Freddie's address into her phone. She was about to lock up when Kevin pulled up outside the gallery. She watched him park his small, yellow Nissan sedan neatly by the kerb. He walked in without saying a word.

'I've been phoning you, Kevin. Didn't you get my messages?'

'I've been busy. What did you want? You haven't sold *North Coast Summers* have you?'

'No, it's not about your painting.'

He looked at her. 'Well, what did you want to talk to me about?'

'I wanted to know if you've seen Freddie Winfred?'

'Freddie? I haven't seen or heard from her since I met her at the Archibald. I've rung her a few times, but all I got was her answering machine. She told me she knew some people who were interested in buying my paintings. I even went around to her gallery, but she wasn't there.'

Jill stared past him and looked out at the traffic on the street.

'Why are you asking?'

'I wanted to speak to her about the exhibition she's got coming up – nothing important.'

Kevin cleared his throat. 'There's something I've got to tell you.'

'What is it?'

'*North Coast Summers*. I want to keep it for sentimental reasons. I don't want to sell it.'

'You sure? I had a cashed up buyer looking at it this morning and I think he's going to buy it.'

'It's not for sale at any price. I've made up my mind.'

'I'll have to check with Bea.' Jill walked to her office and closed the door behind her. A few minutes later, she walked back into the exhibition room.

'Do you want me to bubble wrap it for you?'

Jill stood and watched Kevin drive off and wondered why he had changed his mind about selling the painting. Sentimental reasons? Not likely.

Chapter Nine

Jill checked the address again before she took the steps into the alcove of the red brick apartment block. *Zella (Freddie) Winfred* was typed on a piece of white cardboard behind a small plastic rectangle. She pressed her knuckle against the buzzer marked apartment six. There was no answer. She pressed it again and waited a few moments before she returned to the footpath and found some shade. She was about to text Rimis to ask him what she should do, when a courier pulled up and parked his bicycle against the building. She watched him pull out a large tan envelope from his back pack, check the address and look up at the building, just as she had done only moments before. She followed him into the building's alcove.

'Another scorcher again today,' he said.

'Yeah, what I'd do for a swim.' Jill rummaged through her bag. 'My keys are in here somewhere. Why can't I ever find anything in this bag?'

'My girlfriend has the same problem.' He laughed and pressed the buzzer to apartment four.

'Hello?'

'Cycle courier. Got a delivery for you mate, but you need to sign. You wanna come down or you want me to come up?' The security door clicked. The courier stepped aside to let Jill pass.

'Thanks, found them,' she dangled her house keys in front of him.

Freddie's apartment was at the rear of the block, on the third floor. The balustrade had been recently painted and the tiled stairs smelt of disinfectant.

Jill walked up to the front door of Freddie's apartment and knocked. There was no one about at this time of day. Most people would have been at work. She tried the door handle, but unlike the gallery's back door, it was firmly locked. She turned and looked down the hall before she pulled the lock pick gun from her shoulder bag. Her father had given it to her as a joke for her twenty-first birthday, but it had come in handy over the years, especially a few months ago when she had accidentally locked herself out of her apartment. She looked at the lock. It was an old five-pin tumbler. Easy. The lock slipped back.

'She's not at home, dear.'

Jill froze. She turned her head and looked over her shoulder. The door across the hall was opened and an elderly woman was standing on the threshold with her hands on her hips. She was dressed in a faded floral housecoat, even though it was lunchtime.

'Do you know where she is?'

'I don't think I should be talking to you, my daughter says I shouldn't speak to strangers. You could be a thief, or something worse.'

'It's all right. I'm Freddie's niece, Kylie.'

'What were you doing there with the lock?' The old woman raised her chin in the air and looked at Freddie's door.

'I had a bit of trouble with the key. It was stuck, but I've got the door opened now. See?' Jill stood to one side and pushed the door open with her foot.

'I suppose you look a decent type.' The woman tilted her head to one side. 'Strange, I didn't know Freddie had a niece. She never mentioned you. Thought she only had the one sister, and I'm sure she told me she'd never married.'

'An adopted brother. Auntie Freddie doesn't like to talk about Dad, he's the dark shadow in the family.' Jill shrugged her shoulders. 'You know what families are like.'

'Yes, indeed I do. My mother had a brother who was —'

'So, have you seen Auntie Freddie?'

'She left in a hurry about a week ago,' the woman said.

'What makes you think she left in a hurry?'

'She asked me to drop off some dry cleaning for her, one of her crazy, silk kaftans.' The woman laughed. 'I know they're back in fashion, but I wouldn't be caught dead in one.' She turned to close the door.

'What happened to it?'

'What's that dear?'

'The kaftan?'

'I've still got it. It's hanging up on the back of my bedroom door. Freddie said she'd drop the money into me, but she never did. The dry cleaner likes to be paid up front you see. It's not that I don't trust her, but I didn't want to get caught short.' Before the woman could suggest she take the kaftan herself, Jill went into Freddie's apartment and closed the door.

The apartment was almost identical in size and layout to hers but it had more furniture and was of better quality. A large flat screen TV hung on the far wall while the remaining walls were covered with contemporary art. The kitchen was warm and stuffy, made worse by the smell of burnt coffee and grease. Dirty dishes were stacked in the sink and a cup of untouched black coffee sat on the marble bench top.

Jill opened the kitchen cupboards. She found only the essentials: extra virgin olive oil, green tea, salt and pepper, sugar, a box of toasted muesli. Inside the refrigerator, it was much the same: a milk container past its use by date, a tub of margarine, smoked salmon wrapped up in cling wrap, and a bottle of French champagne, unopened.

Freddie's bedroom was elegant and spacious. It smelled of expensive perfume and the carpet was springy and soft underfoot. The king-size bed was carefully made and she wondered when Freddie had last slept in it. She checked the mattress, the pillows, and under the bed. She walked over to the mirrored robe and slid the doors open. Inside there was a collection of colourful kaftans, half a dozen wraps, even a full length fur coat, a few fancy cocktail dresses, shoes of all descriptions – sandals, low heels, high heels. Freddie's silky kaftans brushed against Jill's bare arms.

Next, she turned to a bank of drawers. Inside the top drawer, she found a neat pile of underwear. She sifted through layers of stockings and slips and found two thick, plain, white envelopes. She opened them and flicked through wads of one hundred dollar notes. She had never seen so much money. The notes were new and crisp and she held them up to her nose to smell the ink. It was then she realised she had forgotten to put gloves on. *Shit*. The woman across the hall had distracted her. Jill pulled a pair from her shoulder bag. How could she have been so stupid? She wiped the notes on the leg of her jeans and returned the money to the drawer. She looked around the room and tried to remember what else she had touched.

She walked into the bathroom. Inside the vanity cupboard she found nothing out of the ordinary: toothpaste, deodorant, a half empty pot of blue eye shadow, and some blusher. She frowned in frustration and tried to pull the pieces of what she knew of Freddie together. If she had 'done a runner,' would she have left her clothing and all her personal items behind? And who in their right mind leaves thousands of dollars in cash in their undies drawer? Jill thought back to the phone left behind at the gallery. And the van. She agreed with the woman across the hall; wherever Freddie was, she had left in a hurry.

Jill stepped back into the bedroom. She noted the empty suitcases and travel bags on the top shelf of the walk-in robe. Next to the robe, stood a small writing desk. An answering machine similar to the one she had seen in Freddie's office was sitting on top of it. She pressed the play button and listened to the recorded messages. She picked up a stack of bank statements, which had been carefully clipped together, and sifted through them. The bank account appeared to be a working account. Cash sums had been deposited at regular intervals. Jill heard his voice and dropped the statements on the desk.

'Freddie, hi, um, it's Kevin Taggart here. Thought we could meet up and have lunch or something. You know, get to know each other a bit better. You've got my number. Gimme a buzz when you get the chance.'

Jill parked her car in a side street and walked the two hundred metres to the Dunworth. She stopped outside the French patisserie and admired the window display. The owner waved to her from behind the counter and she walked into the shop.

'Bonjour, Jean Claude,' she said. 'I haven't enrolled in those French classes yet. Maybe next term, when I've got more time.'

'I can always give you private lessons, *mon cherie*.'

She laughed before she had a chance to wonder if he was serious.

She unlocked the gallery's front door and walked down the hall to her office. She put her feet up onto the desk and pulled a pastry from a white bag. She was about to take a bite, when her phone rang.

'I haven't disturbed you, have I? Hope you're not run off your feet with customers.'

Jill removed her feet from the desk and sat upright in her chair. She hated it when Rimis took this tone with her. Sarcasm didn't suit him, but she knew he hid behind it when he was either frustrated or seriously annoyed. She put her feet back on the desk, tucked the phone into her shoulder and picked at the chocolate filling with the tips of her fingers. 'I'm here on my own. I'm expecting Bea any moment. She's coming in to discuss the final arrangements for the Byron Willis exhibition.'

'Look Brennan, I know you love your new job, but keep your focus on where it's supposed to be, will you?'

Jill pulled a face at the phone. Rimis was always so serious. She wondered what he did in his spare time apart from his crossword puzzles. He was a respected police officer with an impeccable record but he had no family as far as she was aware and few friends, apart from Col Morrissey, his long-time drinking buddy.

'I've been trying to phone you. I think Freddie was being blackmailed. I scanned the note and emailed it to you. Did you get it?' Jill asked.

'Yeah, I got it.'

'What about the reference to *both*? Do you think her sister could be involved?'

'Possibly. Have you been to Freddie's apartment yet?'

'I've just come back from there. I spoke to her neighbour. She hasn't seen her for over a week. Hey, you'll never guess what I found in her undies drawer.'

'Go ahead, surprise me.'

'Wads of cash. At least fifty-thousand dollars in crisp one hundred dollar notes. I wonder if Freddie was up to more than just art fraud?'

Rimis whistled down the phone. 'Anything else?'

'I've been thinking,' Jill said. 'What if Freddie

hasn't run off, and the person who wrote the note has killed her?'

Rimis laughed. 'That's a big leap. What makes you think that?'

'Because everywhere I look, I find evidence of her leaving in a hurry; coffee dregs, unlocked doors, a mobile phone left behind in her office. And then there's the money I found.'

'Maybe she just wants us to believe she left in a hurry. Meet me tonight at Otto's Bar around nine, we'll talk more. And Brennan —'

'Yes, boss?'

'Don't call me, boss.'

Otto's Bar was furnished with small timber tables covered with soggy beer mats. The walls were painted smoky brown, and dusty plastic pot plants crowded every corner. It was nine o'clock sharp when Jill walked in and spotted Rimis and Morrissey sitting up at the bar. Rimis was hunched over his crossword, a glass of red wine in front of him; Morrissey was talking to the barman.

The place gave her the creeps. She knew it was Rimis's favourite watering hole, but she couldn't see the attraction. Otto's was too far from the city centre to attract passing trade and too close to the city to be anyone's local. It relied on occasional university students, cops, and mortuary staff for its trade. She looked around the room and couldn't resist humming the song, *Monster Mash*. It was appropriate in this bar of horrors.

Rimis called her over. Laughter and raised voices swept around the room and carried her towards him.

'You look like you're in a good mood,' Rimis said.

'I was thinking of a song I know.'

'Care to sing a few bars?' Morrissey asked before he gave her the once over.

Jill pulled her shirt down to cover her hips. 'No, it'll keep. How are you anyway, Sarge?'

'No complaints. I was just talking to Nick about the girl washed up at the Baths.' Morrissey dug his fingers into the bowl of nuts on the bar, threw his head back and popped a handful in his mouth. 'I s'pose it won't be long before someone comes forward to claim her. Somebody out there must be missing her, but you never know, do you? Take Freddie Winfred, for example. She could be lying in a ditch somewhere, or off living another life, perfectly happy.' Morrissey swirled the contents of his schooner.

Rimis rolled his eyes.

'What?' Morrissey looked at Rimis. 'Plenty of people go missing every day for all sorts of reasons, or else they die in their homes and nobody thinks about them until the neighbours notice the stench. You know that, Nick, as well as I do.'

Rimis and Jill looked at each other. Jill knew what he was thinking. It had been four days before Rose Phillips' body was found in her kitchen by a real estate agent.

'Want a drink?' Rimis asked Jill.

Jimmy the barman walked up and wiped the bar in

front of them with a red and white checked tea towel. 'What'll it be, love?'

'Soda with ice, thanks. And a slice of lemon if you've got any.'

Morrissey leant over and said to Rimis, 'She's on this detox thing.'

Rimis had a surprised look on his face.

'Hey Nick, you worked out that clue that's been bugging you yet?' Jimmy asked.

Rimis picked up the folded newspaper and looked at the crossword. 'No, not yet, but it'll come. Any good at cryptic crosswords, Brennan?'

'Never tried,' she said.

'Good for the brain; keeps you sharp.'

Jimmy's brother, Tony, was playing the alto sax. The sound was soft, lazy, and with the first low notes, the mood in the place dropped another level.

The soda arrived. Jill took a sip and crunched down on a shard of ice.

'I feel sorry for the old guy who found her,' Morrissey said.

Jill played with her beer mat and listened to the banter between the two men.

'Yeah, it wasn't his day. The shock of it got to him and he ended up at North Shore Hospital. It's not all bad news, though. The dental search came up with a match.'

'Yeah? So who was she?' Morrissey asked.

'We haven't got confirmation yet, but she could be a twenty-year-old student. We need to check with the family, establish next of kin.'

'So, you've got a name?' Morrissey asked.

'Yeah, we think she was Paloma Browne. Strange name.'

Jill coughed and spilt her drink down her jeans. Rimis stared at her. Morrissey threw back his beer and fidgeted on his stool.

'For Christ's sake Brennan, what is it?' Rimis slapped her hard between the shoulder blades. 'You okay?'

She put her glass down on the bar and held up her hand to stop him from hitting her. She reached inside her shoulder bag.

'What've you got?' Rimis said.

She laid the computer-spread sheet on the bar. 'Paloma Browne, under P. Her name is in Freddie's contact list. She could be our blackmailer.'

Rimis stood beside her and looked at the spreadsheet.

Morrisey looked at them. 'What's this about black-mail?'

'I'll tell you about it later,' Rimis said. 'What else you got there?'

Jill looked at Rimis looking at the names. She dropped her shoulder bag to the floor and pulled back on her ponytail. She had both men's attention now.

'Okay. Let's start with Freddie Winfred. She's missing and we're pretty sure she's part of this art racket. But there's someone else in the background. I think there's a good chance it's her sister.' She took a sip of soda water. 'When I was at Freddie's gallery, I saw a Dickerson on the wall. I'm sure it was a fake. I checked the Gallery's website. It was listed for sale at twenty-eight thousand dollars. Then there's the note I found in Freddie's office. If Paloma Browne wrote it, Freddie, or whoever was in this with her, might not have liked the idea of paying up. Maybe they decided to kill her to keep her quiet.' Jill lifted her glass to her lips.

'I can't see Calida Winfred or Freddie having anything to do with murdering the girl,' Rimis said. 'For starters, I don't think they'd have the strength to put her in an industrial bin liner and dump her in the Lane Cove River.'

Morrissey scratched his head. 'It sounds like an open and shut case to me, whichever way you look at it.'

'I think you're being a bit premature, Col,' Rimis said.

'We've got a motive. A case of blackmail gone wrong. One or both of them knock her off, Calida Winfred is tucked away safe and sound in the Hunter Valley, and when Freddie realises we're onto her, she scampers away.'

'Hang on. With respect, Sarge,' Jill said. She saw the look on Rimis's face and wondered what it meant. 'I spoke to the owner of the florist next door to Freddie's gallery. She saw a black Bentley pick Freddie up last Sunday morning. We know Dorin Chisca owns a black Bentley. I can't explain why, put it down to female intuition, but I don't trust him. There's something about him I don't like. He looked nervous when Kevin introduced me as an ex-cop.'

Morrissey nodded at Rimis. 'You want to watch your back with this one, Nick. She'll have your job, if you're not careful.' Morrissey turned away from them and looked down the length of the bar at the two women who had just sat down. They were in their early twenties. One of the women returned Morrissey's look and whispered something in her friend's ear.

Rimis reminded Morrissey that he was married.

'Doesn't hurt to look, Nick.'

Rimis turned back to Jill. 'Anything else?'

'Yeah. William Phillips. He thinks some paintings his company bought from Freddie's gallery are forgeries and he's asked me to take a look at them. It's all coming together, don't you think, boss? I mean, Nick. All these separate bits of information.'

'William Phillips? You mean, Rose Phillips' son?'

'He came to see me at the gallery.'

'Look Brennan,' Rimis said, 'don't let your imagination get too carried away. All we've got is a corpse and a missing person. I think we all agree Freddie Winfred is behind this art fraud business. What we need to do is find her, and quick smart. And go careful with Phillips. I remember the way he used to look at you. I don't want the case compromised.'

Jill opened her mouth and was about to tell him that what she did in her private life was her business, when he looked down at her glass.

'Want another one?'

She shook her head.

'So, where's our mate Taggart then? I don't know if he's got anything to do with Freddie's disappearance, but he's in the picture.'

Jill smiled at Rimis's choice of words. 'I'm meeting him at the gallery tomorrow,' she said. 'At least I think I am. You might want to know, he left a message on Freddie's home answering machine. I checked with the service provider. He was the last person she phoned on the night she was murdered.'

Rimis picked up his glass. He took a mouthful and turned to Morrissey. 'Col, I want you to see what you can find out about Paloma Browne. I want to know what her connection was to Freddie, her sister, Calida, and Dorin Chisca. And find out if she's ever crossed tracks with Kevin Taggart.'

Jill and Morrissey looked at him.

'Taggart?' Morrissey asked.

'Yeah, Taggart. You got a problem with that?'

Morrissey shrugged. 'No, not if you don't.'

'Brennan?'

She shook her head.

Morrissey walked down to the end of the bar. The two women made room for him and he ordered a round of drinks.

Rimis picked up his empty glass. 'Hey, Jimmy, what do you have to do to get a drink around here?' He pulled out a twenty-dollar note and placed it on the bar.

'Time I was heading home,' Jill said. 'It's been a long day. I've got an early start tomorrow.' She pushed her stool back.

'We need a result on this one, Brennan. Sooner rather than later, before it blows up into something none of us bargained for.'

Chapter Ten

The brushed stainless steel doors closed and Jill stood back in one corner of the lift. She watched the buttons light up and waited for the doors to open onto the thirty-ninth floor, the offices of Stockland and Lewis. She was surprised to see William standing at the reception desk, conscious of his eyes on her. She walked the length of the carpeted corridor towards him.

'Sorry I'm late, had a bit of trouble finding a parking space. I should have caught the bus instead.'

Jill was wearing a pair of skin-tight denim jeans and a V-neck sleeveless blouse, one shade darker than Sydney Harbour.

William led her into his corner office and closed the door. She looked around and remembered why she had been infatuated with him when she first met him – there was something about him and this office. There was energy here, order and power. Her attention shifted away from his broad shoulders and narrow hips to the wall behind his desk. 'It's an aquatint with Carborundum,' she said.

'What's that?'

She walked up to the etching and studied it. 'It has

an added technique. Carborundum grit is mixed into a paste and applied to the surface of an aluminium plate.'

'Then what happens?'

'The paste dries. The ink's applied and trapped on the surface, then it's wiped off and printed onto paper in an etching press. What you end up with is a print embossed into the paper.'

'You lost me right after the part where the paste dries.'

Jill laughed. 'Sorry, *La Calebasse* is one of Miró's better examples of the technique.' She pulled her phone out of her bag and read the notes she had made before leaving the gallery.

'Miró sketched it in 1969. It's numbered sixty-six of seventy-five and signed in pencil in the lower right hand corner.' Jill looked at the etching again. 'That stacks up.' She produced a tape measure from her bag and measured the dimensions. 116.8 cm x 83.8 cm. She looked at her notes again.

"What do you think? Is it an original?'

'I'm no expert, but I would say yes. You can usually tell when it comes to art; it's either right or it's wrong, and it looks and feels right to me.' She sighed. 'It's so beautiful, I could stand here and look at it all day.' Jill noticed the look William gave her and tried to ignore it.

'Any idea how much it's worth?' he asked.

'You wouldn't get much change from eighty-thousand, I wouldn't think.'

'Well, that's a relief. The firm paid seventy-four thousand for it three years ago. I hope the Whiteleys and the Brack are genuine. Andy Brogan knows the curator of Australian Art at the Art Gallery. He's coming in to take a look at them later on today. This art fraud business has got everyone nervous.'

Jill turned away from the Miró. William kept a tidy workspace, every file and paper in its place. Dark leather furniture, a massive desk and framed degrees lined the panelled timber walls. She crossed the room to the bank of high windows overlooking Sydney Harbour and looked out. 'Nice view.' An inner Harbour ferry ducked beneath the Bridge and churned its way westward towards Drummoyne. William came up behind her and wrapped his arms around her waist.

Her heart missed a beat. She turned around and looked up into his eyes. He pulled her closer to him and in an instant his lips were on hers. He cupped one of her breasts and breathed deeply.

Her phone vibrated in her pocket and she stepped away from him and took the call.

'So where are you, Brennan? You found Freddie Winfred yet?' Rimis asked.

She took a deep breath, looked at William, and mouthed the word *sorry*. 'On my way back to the gallery now. I'll call you when I get there.'

Jill slid her phone back into her pocket. 'There's someone I have to see this afternoon. I have to go.'

William put his hands on his hips. 'Do you know what you do to me? It's more than a man can stand.'

She laughed. Then blushed. 'Sorry.'

'How about dinner tomorrow night? I know a great Italian place on Campbell Parade.'

'I'm not sure I can make it. I'll call you, okay?' She grabbed her bag and turned back to him.

'Why do I get the feeling you're trying to avoid me? You're always running off somewhere.'

Jill looked at him. 'Look, William. Maybe this is a mistake.'

'What do you mean?'

'The age difference for starters, then there's, well, all this.' Jill looked around the room.

Jill turned her Golf into Queen Street and joined the queue of traffic backed up for almost fifty metres. Women's fashion boutiques, expensive jewellery stores, coffee shops and restaurants lined the route. She turned on the radio, stared ahead at the traffic. Her thoughts were of William. She looked in the rear-view mirror and asked herself, 'Are you, crazy? William is good-looking, educated, wealthy and,' she smiled, 'a great kisser. What sort of woman balks at the chance of going out with a man like that?' A woman like me, she thought to herself.

The traffic began to move and five minutes later she turned the corner into the lane behind Freddie's Gallery. Freddie's van was still parked where it had been the last time she was here. With every day that passed, her disappearance was becoming more disturbing.

Jill had made the decision not to lock the door behind her the last time she was here in case Freddie returned and remembered she had forgotten to lock it. She pulled on her gloves, walked down the hall into

Freddie's office, and returned the SIM card to Freddie's phone.

She slumped into the chair behind the desk and looked down at the bank of drawers beside her. She shook her head. Not going through the desk drawers the last time she was here, not wearing gloves in Freddie's apartment – what other mistakes would she make before this case was solved? She ruffled through the drawers and found nothing of interest in them, apart from a half empty bottle of Highland Park and two glass tumblers.

She tried to push the drawer closed, but it wouldn't go all the way. Something was stuck. She ran her fingers along the back of the drawer. A brass key was taped to the underside of the desk and had worked its way loose. She removed the piece of tape and tapped the key on the desk. It was a safe key.

She looked around the room. The wall opposite her was splashed with colour. The paintings on it were landscapes, except for one, *Nude with Pink Gown*. It was a John Brack and the nude female had her back to her, facing a wall. She stared at it. 'I wonder?' She closed the drawer, crossed the room and lifted the frame.

Yes. She inserted the key in the lock and the door swung open. She pulled out three plastic folders and flipped through the first one. It was all there – audit trails of the art Freddie had bought and sold over the past six months. There was also a list of names, dates, and traceable payments and accounts. A few photocopies of paintings, handwritten notes, yellow stickies. On a sheet of paper, a column headed *Provenance* was underlined. When her eyes flicked down the column, she saw the Miró and the other paintings William and Andy Brogan had been so concerned about. She sighed, relieved for William's sake at least that Stockland and Lewis' art appeared to be genuine.

She turned to the next file. *Innuendos* was scratched in the left hand corner of an A4 sheet of paper. Jill knew Calida Winfred painted innuendos on consignment for Freddie, but there were far too many here to have been painted by her alone. She remembered the conversation she had at Otto's Bar with Rimis and wondered if Paloma Browne was an artist, and if, like Calida Winfred, she had also been painting innuendos for Freddie.

Palm Tree II, a Brett Whiteley screen print, had nine thousand dollars and a question mark next to it. There were also several typed pages of names, addresses, and phone numbers. She put the second file aside.

Inside the third file were neatly typed pages on the gallery's letterhead. She picked up one of the provenance certificates and was surprised by the amount of detail on it. Freddie Winfred knew her stuff. She knew how the art market worked and had the knowledge and skill to create these false certificates. Was she acting alone or was she in partnership with someone? Her sister? Paloma Browne? Did Freddie have anything to do with Paloma's murder and was she off somewhere, enjoying the high life as Morrissey seemed to think?

There was one thing Jill was sure of; Rimis wouldn't stop asking questions until this case was solved. She wanted to find the answers before he did.

Jill scanned the documents with her phone and

when she was satisfied that the room looked exactly as it had before, she returned the safe key to its place at the back of the drawer and rang Rimis.

Rimis walked into his office and sat at his desk. The phone call from Brennan telling him what she had found in Freddie Winfred's gallery should have improved his mood, but he was in anything but good spirits this afternoon. Luke Rawlings and Jenny Choi had been in and out of his office all day with information, but none of it was encouraging. There had been no significant developments in the Browne case. And where was Freddie Winfred? He picked up his newspaper and looked at the crossword clue. Fifteen across: *use some of your gentle ways to persuade them.* He'd been struggling with the clue for the past week.

He gulped down the dregs of his sixth cup of coffee for the day and threw the crossword into the top drawer of his desk. He looked across at the scribbled notes he had jotted down on his writing pad. *KEVIN TAGGART.*

His obsession with Taggart had got him into more trouble with his superiors than he had expected, and he knew what his fellow officers were all saying about him behind his back. Perhaps, they were right. Had he pushed the case against Taggart too hard? At the time of the Blake sisters' deaths, he had requested a twenty-four hour surveillance. When that had been refused, he'd carried out his own surveillance. At the end of his shifts, he would drive to Taggart's house and sit outside in his parked car. Taggart complained to his superiors and Rimis was ordered to stop the harassment.

The findings of the Coroner's inquest into their deaths were that the elderly sisters had died from a combination of too much sherry and carbon monoxide poisoning from a faulty gas heater. The Superintendent told Rimis to take a holiday, which he had flatly refused to do. Rimis knew he couldn't help himself; he'd had a bad feeling about Taggart from the first time he met him.

Rimis read over the notes he had scrawled on the writing pad.

Fact: Kevin Taggart – with his mother when she died from a heart attack. Died on a Sunday.

Fact: Rose Phillips, Taggart's elderly neighbour – murdered six months after Nora Taggart.

He thought about what he had written. Brennan had been right when she'd said that Taggart didn't murder Rose Phillips, Tommy Dwyer did. But who was to say Dwyer didn't beat Taggart to it.

Fact: A month after Rose Phillips' murder – two more deaths in the street. Coroner's report – Blake sisters – sherry, dementia and a faulty heater. Died – Sunday.

Fact: Taggart – financial gain from deaths.

Taggart had been a beneficiary to the estates of all four women and Rimis knew it should have been enough for his superiors to sit up and take notice, but after lengthy questioning, they hadn't been able to break him. He was a devoted son and a model neighbour. He mowed Rose Phillips' lawn for her, invited her in for tea, and had kept a watchful eye out on all his elderly neighbours. Even William Phillips had a few good words to say about him.

Rimis pushed his notes away. His office was on the top floor and faced west. He looked out of the window at the view. He was sure there was a connection between all three deaths. Money? Power? Revenge? Was it a co-incidence Freddie Winfred disappeared less than a week after she met Taggart? Rimis didn't believe in co-incidence. He swung around in his chair, scrawled Freddie's name across his writing pad and underlined it with a thick stroke.

The more he thought about Taggart, the more he was reminded of another case. John Wayne Glover, the Granny Killer.

Glover had been convicted and sentenced to life imprisonment for the serial murders of six elderly women on the North Shore of Sydney in 1990. His file was marked *never to be released*, but fifteen years after he entered Lithgow Gaol, Glover had found his own release by hanging himself.

Rimis's memory rippled back to when he was a nineteen-year-old probationary constable stationed at Lane Cove. The case was his first experience of homicide. It was late afternoon. November, 1989. He and a fellow officer were called to a laneway after a schoolgirl had found an elderly woman's body. The woman was Glover's third victim. She had been struck on the back of the head with a blunt instrument. There were similarities between Taggart and Glover. Similarities that should never have been ignored. Both men were the same age; both had a troubled relationship with older women, in particular, their mother.

The Granny Killer case was unusual. Most serial killers were mentally ill when they committed these acts, but a psychiatrist claimed Glover was sane at the time of the murders. Rimis drummed his pen on the desk. Was Taggart sane? His chain of thought was broken by a knock on the door. It was Morrissey. He walked in and sat down across from Rimis.

'Christ, it's hot in here. What is it with the air con? Can't believe it's broken down again.' Morrissey hooked his finger under his collar and dragged it away from his thick neck.

Rimis crinkled his nose. 'Geez, Col, I can smell you from here. How much did you have to drink last night?'

He shrugged. 'Just a couple.'

'Yeah, right, and the rest. You smell like a brewery.' Rimis tossed a pack of mints across his desk at him. 'What've you found out about Paloma Browne? I'm briefing the Super in an hour. Hope you've got something I can give him?' Rimis wasn't in the mood for Morrissey today.

'No witnesses, no clues.' Morrissey sucked on a mint and flicked through his police issue note pad. It was all for show. Rimis knew he didn't have a single lead to go on. Rimis had recruited extra staff and assigned tasks to all the team members. He knew from experience, most murders solved themselves and were rarely carried out by strangers. Whoever murdered Paloma Browne, it was likely to be someone she knew.

His team had already knocked on all the doors in

the neighbourhood to ask if anyone had seen or heard anything. They had also been over all the statements and re-interviewed everyone with whom they'd spoken when she first went missing, which included the parents. They had drawn a blank. It was disappointing Burns Bay hadn't turned up anything. There were criss-crossing tyre marks, but it was a popular spot. Water samples had been taken and they were hoping for a match with the water found in the girl's lungs. It was a long shot.

'Paloma Browne worked for Freddie Winfred. She was her gallery assistant,' Morrissey said. 'I've asked around. They're usually art students. It's a good way to earn a bit of money on the side, cash in hand.'

'What else you got?'

Morrissey sat back in his chair and reached inside his trouser pocket for his cigarettes.

'Put them away, Col, you know you can't smoke in here.' Rimis thought Morrissey looked pale. Maybe it was the heat. 'What did her friends have to say about her?'

Morrissey drummed his fingers on the cigarette pack. 'A twenty-year-old, street-smart kid, no special boyfriend or girlfriend. Had a bit of a temper on her. Also a bit of a loner. But according to the few friends she did have, she was passionate about her art. Some hint of an involvement with drugs.' He put the cigarettes back in his pocket.

'Dealing or using?'

'Both,' Morrissey said. 'I was told she'd been working long hours on some project she didn't want to talk to anybody about. Told one of her friends her luck was about to change and that she was going to be set for life. I've got Choi and Rawlings and a couple of uniforms at her studio, but so far they haven't found anything. Nothing to suggest what her movements were before she went missing.'

Rimis had a feeling the search of her studio would prove fruitless. If there was anything to indicate what had happened to her, the team would have found something by now. 'So where's her studio?'

'Above a chemist shop in Blues Point Road.'

'McMahons Point?' Rimis wondered how a struggling art student could afford a studio in an exclusive suburb like McMahons Point. It was as if Morrissey read his thoughts.

'It was Brett Whiteley's old stomping ground. She was nuts about him and his work.'

'Was she any good?' Rimis asked.

'What do you mean?'

'Did she have talent?'

'If you want to believe what her lecturers at the Sydney College of the Arts said about her, yeah, she had talent. They told me she had a promising career ahead of her.'

'What did you find out about the family?' Rimis asked.

'Only child. Private school girl but she didn't fit the mould. Her father kicked her out of home when he found a stash of drugs in her bedroom. Parents haven't had contact with her for six months, at least, not until recently, when she got in touch with her mother.' Morrissey shifted in his seat and rubbed the back of his neck.

'How did she afford the rent on the studio?' Rimis asked.

'The parents paid for her college tuition and the studio. Spoilt little rich kid, by all accounts.'

'Anything else I should know?' Rimis was trying to put a picture of the girl together in his mind. He knew the more you knew about the victim, the easier it was to solve the crime.

'No. Nothing else.'

'Might be an idea to contact the media and put her photo out there; see if anyone remembers seeing her around the time she disappeared.'

'It's already on my to-do list. I'll get Chapman onto it.' Morrissey stood to leave. 'Do we know how she died?'

'I spoke to Doctor Ross this morning. She's still waiting for the tox reports to come back before she commits to anything. The Lab's running a few weeks behind, so we might be waiting a while. She's thorough, I'll give her that.'

'What about Freddie Winfred?' Morrissey asked. 'Think she's got anything to do with the girl's murder?'

'Let's ask her when we find her. I also want to know if Taggart knew her. If she was Freddie's assistant, he might have met her, taken a liking or a disliking to her. Kevin has this thing for older women, but it could be worth having a look at just the same.'

'You want me to go see him? Put the hard word on him?'

'No, let him be for the moment. Brennan's got her eye on him.'

There was a knock at the door. Morrissey turned around.

'Well, what is it Rawlings?' Rimis asked.

'Thought you'd want to know boss. It's the Winfred woman. They've found her.'

Chapter Eleven

It's the smell he notices first. The stench, like rotting garbage, is ripe and slightly sweet. He flicks on a grubby light switch on the wall by the loading dock. The industrial lights flicker and clunk and light up the warehouse like a convenience store. He looks at the floor-to-ceiling racking. Empty shelves, apart from a few boxes. He strolls about the warehouse with his hands in his pockets, whistling quietly to himself. He sniffs at the air, shifts a cardboard box and looks behind it. He wonders if an animal has become trapped in here, a ringtail possum, or a rat, perhaps. He unlocks the storeroom and walks inside. The narrow windows are sealed and the dusty grey venetian blinds are shut tight. He weaves his way through the Roberts, McCubbins, and Streetons. There isn't a piece of wall or carpet that's not covered in canvases. He wants to start shifting stock, but he knows he has to wait until the next shipment arrives. It should have been here two days ago and he is running out of time. He looks across at North Coast Summers*; it is still wrapped in bubble wrap and is sitting in the corner of the room.*

He walks out into the warehouse. There's that smell again. He decides it's coming from the bathroom.

He pushes the door open and lifts his forearm to cover his nose. The smell of excrement is overpowering. He flicks the light switch and remembers he didn't replace the blown bulb the last time he was here.

The smell is even stronger now and he curses at the thought of having to call the plumber. The last thing he needs is another set of prying eyes around the place.

His eyes dart around the small room. He notices the up-turned red plastic bucket in the corner, the puddles of water on the blue floor tiles. He opens the door to the toilet stall and recoils in horror. He puts both hands over his mouth, holds his breath and looks at the silky kaftan pooled around her body, carefully arranged like a posy of brightly coloured flowers. He tries to avoid looking at her legs, the lumpy flesh, slack on the bone, mottled with bruises. The colours remind him of springtime in Bucharest; the pale mauves, pinks and yellows; they are the colours of his childhood.

The ambulance doors slammed shut. Rimis and Brennan walked out from the warehouse and into the sunlight. Rimis knew Doctor Ross would be wondering what it was about the North Shore of Sydney. Since starting the job, there had been two homicides within weeks of each other and Doctor Ashleigh Taylor, the city's Chief Forensic Pathologist, not around for either of them.

Doctor Ross had arrived from Cape Town two

months ago. When Rimis first met her, he had tried to imagine what had brought her halfway around the world. There was no ring on her wedding finger or a mark to suggest there ever had been. He guessed she was around his age, late thirties. With big, round eyes and smooth dusky skin, it was easier for him to imagine her in some smart North Sydney advertising agency than in a mortuary. What was the appeal, he wondered? What on earth did death and a woman like Greer Ross have in common?

'Fractured skull, possible drowning,' she said to Rimis when he asked her the cause of death. 'She either fell or was pushed before her head was rammed down the toilet bowl. I'll have to run tests to make sure the water in the lungs match the toilet water.'

'Time of death?' Rimis asked.

'At least a week.'

'Any signs of a struggle?'

'There's bruising on the arms and wrists. I'd expect the perp to have scratches, if that's any help. I've bagged the hands and taken skin samples from beneath the fingernails.' She handed a clipboard to Rimis. 'If you could countersign here, Inspector, my report should be ready early next week, but don't hold me to it. With Doctor Taylor interstate, we don't have enough staff to handle the back-log, let alone the extra work load.'

Doctor Ross returned to her car. Rimis watched the sway of her hips and wondered why she had given him such an icy reception.

'What's her problem?' Rimis asked Brennan.

'Sounds like she's overworked.'

'I know what that feels like,' he raised his eyebrows. 'With Freddie dead, it's time to put your resignation in at the Dunworth. And here was I thinking this was going to be a straightforward case.' He looked over at a couple of reporters and a photographer talking to some bystanders. 'Those lot have been sniffing around for a story on this art fraud business for months. Looks like they've struck it lucky – two for the price of one.'

'So, what do we do now?' Jill asked.

'Let's find out what Chisca has to say for himself.'

They walked towards the loading dock. Chisca was standing next to a female uniformed officer. He had a lit cigarette in one hand, a mobile phone in the other. He was dressed casually in a pair of beige chinos. Curly sprigs of black chest hair poked out from his white polo shirt.

'Mr Chisca. I'm Detective Inspector Rimis, from Chatswood Detectives, and this is Senior Constable Brennan.'

They flashed their ID at him. Chisca took a slow, long drag on his cigarette and stubbed the spent butt on the floor with the ball of his shoe.

'I have to go,' Chisca whispered down the phone in a heavy accent. He ended the call and returned the phone to his trouser pocket.

'Quite a shock for you this morning,' Rimis said. 'Mind if we ask you a few questions?'

'No, I do not mind.' Chisca looked at Brennan and smiled. 'We have met before. It was at the Archies.'

'You have a good memory,' she said.

'And you are a police officer. A police officer who knows a lot about art.'

'I know a lot about many things, Mr Chisca.'

'So, this is your warehouse?' Rimis looked around him.

'I do not own it. I rent it.'

'We'll need the landlord's details. Do you know if he's got a key?

Chisca shrugged his shoulders. 'I do not think so.'

Rimis walked into the warehouse and stood with his hands in his trouser pockets. He looked up and down the length of the warehouse and at the racking. He noticed the empty shelves. Chisca and Brennan followed.

'It's a bit empty, isn't it? Waiting for more stock to arrive?'

'I'm returning to Romania at the end of the week. I'm going home to look after my elderly parents.'

'Oh, I see. That's a fine thing, a son looking after his parents. Don't you agree, Senior?'

'It certainly is, Sir. Very commendable.'

'Can I ask what line of business you're in, Dorin? You don't mind if I call you Dorin, do you?' Rimis asked.

Chisca shrugged his shoulders again, a habit which was beginning to annoy Rimis. He flipped opened a silver cigarette case and lit another cigarette, drew on it and exhaled slowly. He blew the smoke towards them. Rimis drew in the tobacco and remembered how hard it had been to give up.

'Would you like one?'

'No, everyone knows they stunt your growth.'

Brennan stifled a laugh.

'So what line of business you in, Dorin?'

'I had two businesses. Plumbing supplies, my bread

and butter, I think this is the term, and an art invest-ment business. I supplied innuendoes to companies and private individuals.' Chisca looked at Rimis. 'Do you know what I mean by this word, innuendo?'

'Yes, indeed I do.'

'This is terrible, terrible business. Freddie Win-fred was such a fine woman. Who would do such an undignified thing to her?'

'What was she doing here, anyway? Got any ideas?' Rimis cast his eye around the warehouse.

'I don't know.'

'How did she get in? Did she have a remote control to the roller shutters?'

'Now that I think of it, yes she did. I meant to ask her to return it to me but it slipped my mind.'

'What about the storeroom?'

'Only I have a key, but there is a spare in my office. It's in the top drawer, in a brown envelope.'

'Brennan, check it out.'

Brennan nodded and walked down the length of the aisle to the office. Rimis watched her go then turned his attention back to Chisca. 'When you arrived, was the storeroom locked?'

'Yes.'

'And what about security? Is there an alarm sys-tem?'

'Yes, we have an alarm. Freddie knew the code. It is a simple number, easy to remember. 1234.'

Rimis was indeed surprised by its simplicity. '1234?' He looked at Chisca and raised his eyebrows.

'When something is obvious Inspector, we often do not see what is under our very noses.'

'You're probably right.' Rimis remembered his crossword puzzle.

'Couldn't find the key, boss.'

'Can I ask what your relationship with Freddie Winfred was?' Brennan pulled out her note pad, pushed her sunglasses to the top of her head and squinted.

'Freddie and I were business partners. I do not believe in mixing business and pleasure. It is a lesson learnt many years ago.'

Brennan remembered the way Freddie had looked at him at the Archibald and wondered if he was telling the truth. 'Was she involved in your business financially?'

'No.'

'Did you have any involvement in the Winfred Gallery, financially or otherwise?'

'No, I did not.'

'Have you ever met Calida Winfred?'

'No, I have not had that pleasure. She lives in the country I believe. In the Hunters Valley.'

'Hunter Valley,' Rimis corrected him.

'You must have heard Freddie talk about her?' Brennan asked.

'Yes, of course. Freddie was proud of her sister. Calida Winfred has produced many fine works in her career, including a number of innuendos she painted for me on consignment.'

'Seems a waste of talent painting these innuendos, don't you think?' Rimis asked.

'I heard there was a fire and she is not the person she once was. Perhaps she lost confidence in her ability.'

'Let's get back to your relationship with Freddie and her role in the business,' Rimis said.

'Inspector, Freddie was the front man.'

'You mean she was the first point of contact?'

'Yes, she was the face behind the business. She was outgoing and people liked her.' Chisca twisted his heel on the stub of the cigarette. 'If you have finished with your questions I would like to go home. I am upset by what has happened here.'

'We've finished for now, but we'll need you to come down to the station to give a full statement. Does tomorrow suit?'

Chisca nodded.

'Our people have finished, but I should remind you, this is still a crime scene and we'd appreciate your co-operation.' Rimis turned to Brennan. 'I want an officer here for the next forty-eight hours.' Brennan nodded and Rimis turned his attention to the exhibit officer in charge. He watched him remove his protective overalls and stow them in the boot of his car. Rimis knew an exhibits officer was not a popular job. It involved keeping track of every piece of evidence at the crime scene and maintaining a record of continuity.

Rimis turned back to Chisca and handed him his card. A sleek, black Bentley drove into the car park and parked in one of the spaces marked *Chisca Plumbing Supplies*. A man got out.

'If you think of anything that could help us in our enquiries, you can contact me on this number, 24/7.'

Chisca tucked the card in his shirt pocket and walked towards the parked car.

Rimis looked at both men as they stood together. Chisca appeared upset, had his hand on the man's shoulder and was talking to him quietly. He was a crude, thick-set man, a few centimetres shorter than Chisca. He dug his hands into his armpits and looked over at Rimis and Brennan.

Rimis and Brennan walked up to them. Rimis noticed Chisca's minder had *HATE* tattooed between both sets of knuckles. He looked like a boxer – a thick neck and a nose that looked as if it had been broken more than once.

'This is Nicolae Vladu, my personal assistant. Nicolae, this is Inspector Rimis and Senior Constable Brennan, they are investigating Freddie's death.'

'Nice to meet you, Mr Vladu.'

Vladu nodded and looked down at his tattooed hands.

Rimis removed his sunglasses and looked at the Bentley. 'Nice set of wheels you've got here, Dorin. I've never had a black car; always thought they showed the dirt.' Rimis ran the flat of his hand across the shiny bonnet. Vladu scowled, removed a clean handkerchief from his trouser pocket and wiped away Rimis's hand marks. He opened the passenger door for Chisca, waited for him to be seated, then walked around to the driver's door.

Rimis squatted down and spoke to Chisca through the open window. 'We'll see you tomorrow then, Dorin. Morning, before lunch, is better for me.' Vladu started the engine. 'One more thing,' Rimis said. 'Freddie's gallery assistant, Paloma Browne. You ever meet her?'

'Freddie never mentioned her to me and, no, I have never met her.'

Rimis and Brennan watched Vladu reverse the Bentley out of the narrow car space.

'He's a showy type of fella, our Mr Chisca. Likes to display his wealth, doesn't he?' Rimis said.

Rimis dropped Brennan back at the Station and headed north on the Pacific Highway. He knew they would have to move quickly. The press were going to have a field day with the story when it broke. He could see the headlines now. *Gallery Owner and Assistant, Murdered.* The cases were now his number one priority; everything else on his desk would have to wait.

He took the ramp north onto the M1. He pulled down the sun visor. The traffic was light, apart from a few interstate semi-trailers. He overtook the truck ahead of him but braked hard when he spotted a speed camera.

Rimis knew he could have sent one of his underlings to tell Calida Winfred her sister was dead, but he liked the woman, and out of respect for her and Ted Mackie, he knew it was only right that they hear the bad news from him. He thought about the indignity of Freddie's death. No one should have to die like that.

By the time he parked his car, it was early afternoon. He looked towards the croquet lawn and recognised Ted Mackie immediately. He was hard to miss, being the tallest of the group. It was Ted's turn to play a shot. He swung his mallet and gently hit the red ball. It passed through the hoop and Ted pushed back the aviator shades onto his head and placed his hands on his hips. He was wearing one of his Hawaiian shirts again. The sleeves were short and they revealed a pair of strong arms. Sturdy tanned legs poked out from beneath a pair of red cargo pants and his thick calves were covered with wiry sprigs of greyish, blonde hair. Ted spotted Rimis and walked up to him. 'Didn't expect to see you back so soon. You've got some news. Bad, by the look of it.'

'Yeah, it's not good.' Rimis gave a report of what had happened to Freddie. During their careers, both men had had their share of delivering bad news. The *death message* was a sobering experience and it never got any easier, no matter how many times you did it.

They walked across the lawn together in silence.

'You ever miss the job, Ted?'

'Not one bit. After Mary died, I realised I still had a lot of living to do and that's exactly what I plan to do.'

Ted walked up to the reception desk and asked Jasmine if he had seen Calida.

'Hello, Ted, and hello again, Inspector.' She leaned forward on her elbows. 'I saw her on her way to the arts and crafts room after lunch. I think she's still there.'

The two men crossed the reception area and made their way in silence to the eastern wing of the building. The smell of overcooked vegetables and lamb followed them down the corridor.

'You want to tell her, or do you want me to?' Ted asked. Ted tapped lightly on the door and looked at Rimis.

'I'll do it,' Rimis said.

'Who is it?'

'Cal, it's me, Ted. I've got DI Rimis here with me.'

Calida opened the door. Rimis smelt linseed oil and turpentine.

'How about we go to your room, Cal,' Rimis said.

Calida dipped a paintbrush in a glass of muddy-coloured water, removed it and wiped the bristles clean with a rag. She took off her painting smock and threw it on a chair. Rimis and Ted followed behind her down the corridor towards her room.

'Now then, what news of Freddie? I assume that's why you have come.'

'You might want to sit down, Cal,' Ted said.

'I'm alright, Ted. I'd prefer to stand to hear what Inspector Rimis has to say.'

Rimis looked at her and tried to frame a gentle way to tell her, but he knew from experience there was no way to relate bad news, other than to come right out and say it. 'Cal, Freddie's dead.'

Both men heard her catch her breath. Ted guided her to an armchair. The window was open about eight centimetres and Rimis heard a ride-on lawn mower, laughter from the croquet lawn, and a far-off crow, shrieking.

'You're certain then?'

'No mistake,' Rimis said.

'I told you, didn't I, Ted? I knew something had happened to her. I'd almost resigned myself to it.' Calida sat down and picked up a framed photograph from the window sill. 'This was taken in front of the ferris wheel at the Royal Easter Show.' She ran her fingers over the photo. 'Freddie was six years old, I was sixteen. It was the first year Dad let me drive the dodgem cars. I can still remember the sparks flashing off the high poles and Freddie telling me to drive faster. Typical Freddie,' she smiled. Calida's eyes filled with tears but she made no attempt to wipe them away. Rimis was still standing by the door. She looked over at him. 'Was it her heart, Inspector? Is that what killed her? I don't remember how many times I told her to do something about her weight, and the drinking. She was always drinking.'

Rimis walked over, knelt down in front of her and took her hands in his.

'She didn't have a heart attack, Cal.'

'If it wasn't her heart, then what was it?'

It was a difficult question for Rimis to answer. He didn't have it in him to tell her she drowned in a toilet bowl. That piece of information would be best saved for another day.

'Drowned,' he said.

'That's not possible,' she looked at him, her eyes wide. 'Freddie was a good swimmer. She always won the age races at school.'

'I have to tell you –'

'Tell me what, Inspector?'

'We're treating Freddie's death as suspicious.'

Calida's face crumpled. 'Sweet Jesus. What are you

saying? She was murdered?' A hand went to her mouth. Ted moved to her side but she waved him away.

'Take a few deep breaths, Cal.' Ted said. 'Do you want me to call for the nurse?'

'No, I'm alright. It's the shock.' Tears were running down her flushed cheeks. She removed a handkerchief from her sleeve.

'It doesn't make sense. Who in the world would want to hurt Freddie?' Calida stood up from the chair and wiped her eyes.

'I don't know. I can't tell you that,' Rimis said. 'Was there anything bothering her? Can you think of anyone who would have wanted to harm her? I'm sorry to have to ask you these questions.'

Calida didn't hesitate. 'Definitely not. Everyone loved Freddie. Of course, there were people who thought she was a little loud, eccentric even, but –'

'Think back to the last time you saw her. Do you remember the conversation you had with her? Did she mention anyone you hadn't heard her speaking about before?' Rimis asked.

Calida had calmed down a little now. 'I have no idea what kind of people she dealt with. She didn't discuss her clients with me.'

'Try to think,' Ted touched her arm.

'There was that fellow she met at the Archibald. He was the winner of the Wynne Prize last year. She liked his work. She did tell me his name, but I've always been terrible with names. I think it was Kevin, someone or other.'

'Kevin Taggart,' Rimis said.

'Yes, that was it. She phoned me and told me she

had met him. She didn't like him. She told me there was something strange about him. You don't think he murdered her do you?'

'Anyone else?' said Rimis, ignoring her question.

'No, I can't think of a single soul who would want to harm her.' Calida wiped her eyes.

Rimis looked at her closely.

'Did Freddie ever mention a Romanian art dealer by the name of Dorin Chisca?'

Calida was staring out of the window now with her back to Rimis and Ted.

'Cal, did you hear what Inspector Rimis asked you? 'Who did you say?'

Rimis repeated Chisca's name.

Calida turned around. 'Dorin Chisca? No. I've never heard of him.'

'You seem quite sure,' he said.

'Of course I'm sure. Freddie was a very private type of person, Inspector; she kept everything close to her chest, strictly on a need-to-know basis. Why are you asking about this Dorin Chisca?'

'We have reason to believe Freddie was involved in an art fraud scam operating out of Sydney. She was passing off your innuendos as originals.'

'What?' Calida looked at Rimis with wide eyes. 'I don't believe you. Freddie would never get involved in anything illegal.' Calida got to her feet and wrapped her arms around her chest. 'Now, if there isn't anything else, I think you should leave. I've had enough bad news for one day.'

'I'm leaving now, but there's another matter. I know

this has been a shock for you Cal, but we need your consent to search Freddie's gallery and apartment.'

Calida walked over to her bedside drawer and opened it. She pulled out a set of keys and handed them to Rimis. 'Here, take these and I'll give you anything else you need. Just find whoever killed Freddie.'

Rimis took the keys. 'Because you're the next of kin, I also have to ask if you can identify your sister's body. We can ask someone else if —'

'No, she's my sister; it's proper I do it.' She tucked her handkerchief up her sleeve. Rimis looked at her before he turned to leave. The room was full of misery and he knew it wouldn't be long before the anger set in.

Chapter Twelve

Jill lived in Bondi in one of four Art-Deco apartments on New South Head Road. It was up two flights of stairs on the second floor. The rent was more than she could afford, but she was prepared to pay it because it was within walking distance of Bondi Beach. It was one of the nicest places she had ever lived.

Jill was in the bathroom putting the final touches to her make-up when she heard the knock at the front door. She quickly applied some lipstick and took one last look in the mirror. She didn't normally wear make-up, her complexion was clear enough that she could get away with only wearing tinted SPF 30 sunscreen. She combed her fingers through her hair. She had decided to wear it out tonight instead of tying it back in a ponytail. The heels she was wearing added another five centimetres to her height. Her father had told her she took after her mother's side of the family in the height department. In her stocking feet she stood at one hundred and sixty-five centimetres.

She removed the brass security chain and opened the door. She stepped back, but before she had a chance to say anything, he pulled her to him. She closed her eyes and he kissed her. He wrapped his arms around her and then his hot breath was on her neck. He kissed her again, touched her hair and throat. Intimate. Maybe it might work out between them after all.

'You're beautiful,' he said.

She pulled away from him. Her face blushed and she waved him into the only armchair in the room. She hoped he wouldn't notice the grease stains on the arms. She should have told him to sit on the lounge instead.

Before William arrived, she had run the vacuum cleaner over the floorboards and had even thought to pick up a bunch of gardenias from the greengrocers on her way home, but they had been a mistake. The scent was overpowering in the confines of the small apartment. 'I'll get us something to drink. Red wine okay?' She said.

She went into the kitchen and grabbed an open bottle of Shiraz from the bench, and two large wine glasses. When she returned to the lounge room he was standing, looking at the art on the walls. 'You painted these?'

She nodded.

'They're very good.'

'You're just being polite. I painted them when I was at University.' She put the wine and the glasses down on the coffee table, walked up to him and stood by his side. 'They're technically competent I suppose, but I lack what it takes to make a great artist. Kevin Taggart on the other hand, has no formal training, yet he has passion, vision. He's a genius.'

'I was impressed by his latest works, but what about you? Are you still painting?' he asked.

'Wish I had the time. I used to go down to the beach with my sketchpad before I took over at the gallery. I keep promising myself I'll enrol in life drawing classes, but something always seems to get in the way.'

'Life's like that. What was it that John Lennon said? Life is what happens to you while you're busy making other plans.'

'You're a Beatles fan?' Jill asked.

'Yeah, got all their albums. Grew up playing them on my old 45 record player.'

'I wasn't even born when John Lennon died and I don't even know what a 45 record looks like,' Jill said.

'What are you trying to do, make me feel old?'

'Not at all, old man.' Jill laughed. 'Come and sit down.' She poured him a glass of wine. She had planned to tell him after dinner but changed her mind. She knew it would be better if he heard the truth from her, rather than finding out about it in the morning papers. 'William, there's something I have to tell you.' She filled her glass and sat down on the ottoman opposite him.

'Sounds serious,' he said.

Jill took a mouthful of wine. It brought colour to her cheeks. She fell silent for a moment, then she looked up at him. 'Did you hear about the woman they found in the warehouse in Chatswood today?'

'I heard it on the news on the way over here.'

'And the girl washed up at Woolwich Baths?' She said in a quiet voice.

'I remember reading something about it in the

papers.' He leant over and put his glass down on the coffee table. 'Where are you going with all this? You've left the police.'

Jill took another mouthful of wine. 'The two women are thought to be involved in this art fraud racket that's been in all the papers and that everyone's been talking about.' Jill looked down at her hands and picked at her nails. 'You remember, Nick Rimis?'

'Of course I do. Funny you should mention him; he came to see me the other day about Kevin. He gave me his card and was asking all sorts of questions about my mother and the Blake sisters. He's convinced Kevin had something to do with their deaths and told me if Tommy Dwyer hadn't killed my mother, Kevin would have. I couldn't believe he said that to me, after everything Kevin did for the elderly women in the street.'

'Nick Rimis takes his cases seriously. I think in some way he holds himself responsible for those women's deaths.' She saw the puzzled look on his face.

'So, he's working on this art fraud business then?'

'We're working on it together.'

'Together? What are you talking about?'

'I was assigned to a special task force to help with the investigation because of my art background.' Jill looked at him. 'I haven't resigned from the service.'

William got to his feet. 'What the hell are you talking about?' There was anger in his voice.

'I haven't resigned. I was working at the Dunworth as an undercover operative.'

'Are you serious?'

She stood up from the ottoman. 'I had to immerse myself completely in the assignment and convince everyone that I was the assistant director of the Meghan Dunworth Gallery. Not even Bea Travers knew.'

Silence.

William looked at her. Frown lines appeared on his forehead. 'I hope you find whoever killed those two women.' He stood and put his empty glass down on the coffee table. 'And thanks for the wine. You'll understand if I don't take you to dinner. I've lost my appetite.'

Jill stared at him. No, she didn't understand why he had changed his mind about taking her to dinner. During the investigation into his mother's murder, Jill had learnt that Rose Phillips had lied to him about who his father was and that his birth mother had given him up to Rose Phillips to raise. Perhaps that was why he was so sensitive to any form of deception.

Jill leaned on the balustrade and watched him leave. She wanted to run after him but she knew she should let him go.

'Good luck saving the world,' he called out on his way down the stairs. She expected him to turn around, to apologise, and to tell her he had been caught off guard, but he didn't look back. She listened to his footsteps as they thumped down the stairs. The last sound she heard was the shudder of glass in the lobby door.

Jill walked back into her apartment and dropped onto the sofa. She picked up the bottle of wine and refilled her glass to the brim. She thought about phoning Rimis for a reason she didn't quite understand, but decided against it. What would he say to her? He had told her William Phillips was bad news from the start, and he had been right. She should have listened to him and left William alone. She emptied her third glass of wine and knew if she didn't find some balance in her life, she would end up like Rimis.

It could have been the alcohol or the maudlin state she was in, but she couldn't stop herself from thinking about her father. He was the most decent and kind-hearted man she had ever known. Morrissey's description didn't match the memory she had of him. Morrisey said her father had been hot-headed, had a quick temper. She remembered his outbursts, but she had been a difficult teenager, hadn't she?

She poured herself another glass of wine and knew she needed more than ever to understand what happened four years ago in Lakemba. She staggered to the bookcase and picked up the photo of her parents on their wedding day. They looked so right together, but she knew the timing had always been wrong for the Brennans.

Chapter Thirteen

Rimis made a bad job of parking his car in the loading zone in front of the newsagent. He grabbed a copy of the Sydney Morning Herald and looked at the front page. The media had reacted quickly, just as he had expected, and were milking this for all it was worth.

ART FRAUD TURNS TO MURDER.

The body of a 58-year-old woman was found in a warehouse in Chatswood yesterday morning. The deceased was Zella Winfred, an eastern suburbs art gallery owner and socialite. She was also at the centre of an undercover police investigation into an art fraud racket operating in Sydney. Her business associate, Mr Dorin Chisca, found her body. Anyone with information is asked to contact Chatswood Detectives…

Under the headline was a photo of the warehouse, in the background, Chisca's Bentley. Rimis knew if he could be bothered to turn the radio on, he would hear the full story on the seven a.m. news. He walked into Chatswood Station thirty minutes later feeling that it was going to be another frustrating day. He threw the newspaper onto his desk and turned to the back pages, tore out the day's cryptic crossword and clipped it to the others in the top drawer of his desk. That damn clue was still on his mind. Fifteen down. He couldn't even begin to think of starting on another crossword until he'd solved the one he was working on.

At eight-thirty, his phone rang. He had thought about switching it to voicemail when he'd arrived this morning, but he'd been distracted and forgotten all about it.

'Rimis,' he barked down the line. He leant forward and listened carefully to what the caller was saying. A few minutes later, he stood up from his desk and grabbed his jacket.

Brennan tapped on the door.

'Boss, I was —' She had a black ring file in one hand and a cup of coffee in the other. She was about to sit down but she must have noticed the look on his face.

'Not now, Brennan. I'll be back in a few hours. Come and see me then.'

She followed him out of his office.

'Brennan. There you are,' Rawlings called down the corridor. Luke Rawlings was a snappy dresser. Today he was wearing a dark navy Oxford jacket, a white cotton shirt, and a pale blue silk tie. 'We've flipped for it. It's your turn to get the coffee.' He looked at the cardboard cup in her hand.

'Oh, come on Luke. I did the coffee run yesterday.

And anyway, what's wrong with the coffee from the canteen? I'm drinking it, aren't I?'

'Don't know how you can drink that dishwater. Come on, be a good sport.' She looked up at him. He smiled at her. He was tall and shambling. His wavy blonde hair was expertly gelled; he smelt of expensive after-shave and he had the deepest blue eyes she had ever seen. No wonder he had a reputation with the female officers.

'Don't forget, I like my cappuccino extra hot and with lots of chocolate on top,' he said, before heading back into the main incident room.

Five minutes later, Jill was on Archer Street. It was a warm morning, the traffic was heavy and the footpath was crowded with the usual mix of shoppers and office workers. She walked into Cafe New York. The cafe smelt of fresh coffee, toast, melted cheese and bacon. She placed the order, with Luke's requests. As an afterthought, she ordered two almond biscuits for herself. She leant against the counter while she waited.

'Jill.' The coffees were on the bench next to the cash register. The young woman behind the counter smiled at her. She was tall, with long honey-blonde hair; Jill had her pegged as a university student. Jill remembered her own university days and the financial struggle, the study and the shift work as a Coles checkout chic in Maroubra.

'Coffee.' Jill announced five minutes later, placing the cardboard carrier on her desk in the incident room.

'Thanks.' Morrissey winked at her and grabbed his

extra-large macchiato. He creaked the plastic lid off his coffee.

'We should get a decent coffee machine, Sarge. It would save on unnecessary down time.'

'You're probably right, Brennan. I'll speak to the boss about it; see if we've got anything left over on this month's budget. Money's tight right now with the overtime we've all been putting in.'

'Speaking of the boss, any idea where he went this morning in such a hurry?' Jill asked.

Morrissey looked at her. 'Haven't got a bloody clue.'

Chapter Fourteen

Jill unlocked the door to her apartment, walked into her bedroom and kicked off her shoes. The desk in the corner was scattered with unpaid bills, a writing pad, and an open police procedural manual. Her shift had finished at midnight. She should go straight to bed, but she knew she wouldn't sleep. Adrenalin was still pumping through her veins. She changed into a pair of pink boxer shorts and an over-sized T-shirt and sat down at her desk.

She flicked through the police manual and began revising the standard operating procedures for detaining someone after an arrest. The next time she looked across at her clock radio on the bedside table it was two a.m. She yawned, ran her fingers through her hair and walked out into the kitchen. The kitchen was so small that only a few steps were needed to make it to the sink. She filled the electric jug, waited for the water to boil and poured herself a cup of green tea. She carried the mug back to her bedroom and sat down on her chair, tucking her legs under her. The computer screen came to life and she remembered what Rimis had told her about John Wayne Glover. She Googled the *Granny Killer*.

Rimis told her Glover had been a volunteer at the local senior citizens centre, was married with two daughters, and had led a pathetically ordinary life. She clicked on *Wikepedia*. It gave details of his killing spree and his background. Glover had built-up aggression and hostility towards his mother, and when she'd died, he'd needed to take it out on someone. What she read was both horrifying and sad. Jill hit the shut-down command and closed her laptop.

It was still dark when she opened her eyes a few hours later. She rolled over, kicked off the bed sheet. Even with the window open, the room was hot and airless. She tried willing herself back to sleep but it was no use. She padded barefoot into the kitchen and opened the fridge door, staring into the cool empti-ness. There was nothing there except for two bottles of wine and a furry pack of bacon. She really must do some shopping. She closed the fridge door and went back to bed.

Jill was one of the first to arrive at the Station the following morning. She nodded at Rimis when she passed his office.

'Good to see you in so early, Brennan,' he said.

'Couldn't sleep.' She walked down the corridor to the Major Incident Room. It was mushroom brown, someone's attempt to make it look up-to-date and modern. There was a joke about mushrooms, some-thing about being fed bullshit and kept in the dark. It wasn't far from the truth. She wasn't getting anywhere with all the paperwork stacked up on her desk. She sat down and looked around the room. It was littered with printouts, dusty boxes, ring binders, over-flowing in-trays and files. She wished she could open a window; the room was stale, laced with the remains of yesterday's take-away lunches, spicy peanuts, old coffee, sweat and frustration. She flipped through the files in front of her and read them selectively, using a pink high-lighter to mark information she thought was important or relevant.

Detectives Jenny Choi and Matt Chapman arrived twenty minutes after her. Jenny Choi was efficient and had an eye for detail. She was also the liaison officer for the local Chinese community. Jill hadn't had a chance to get to know her, but remembered how Jenny had gone out of her way to make her feel welcome when she'd first arrived. Matt Chapman, on the other hand, had a reputation around the station as a general dogs-body and a bore. He hadn't offended anyone or screwed up as far as Jill had heard, but he lacked initiative.

They both had their heads down at their desks on the other side of the room, taking and making calls, drinking coffee and scouring the boxes of paper files from Freddie's office and from Paloma Browne's studio. They were doing the legwork, trying to establish profiles for both women, deciding who should be questioned. It wouldn't be long before forensic reports and witness statements would start arriving. The public also needed to know what phone numbers to ring if they had any information.

There was a morning meeting scheduled for ten-thirty, but Rimis had postponed it to later in the day. Jill had already noticed his short absences and wondered what was going on in his life. A woman? Family issues? It couldn't be family; Rimis didn't have one as far as she knew. As for women, Nick Rimis had only one love in his life, and that was his job.

A line of perspiration tracked across her forehead and dripped down the side of her face. The air conditioning had broken down again, but thankfully, pedestal fans had been requisitioned and were due to arrive sometime today. Jill tucked a stray strand of hair behind one ear and looked at the red roses William had sent her. She had been embarrassed when the duty sergeant had called her down to collect them from the front desk this morning. They had already begun to wilt because of the heat. Why didn't she just throw them in the bin? It was over between them, over before it had even started. She sighed, refreshed the computer screen and picked up a file.

'Brennan?'

Jill jumped. 'You shouldn't sneak up on someone like that, Sarge. You scared me half to death.'

Col Morrissey looked over her shoulder. She saw him looking at the roses. He sat down on the corner of the desk and looked around the room.

She smelt traces of tobacco and stale beer on his breath.

He suddenly stood up and walked over to the water cooler and filled a cup with filtered water. She saw him looking at the forensic photos of Paloma.

'Scott Carver. He's your cousin, isn't he?' Jill asked.

He turned around and looked at her. 'Yeah and like

me, he's charming and good-looking, but he works too hard. Doesn't get out much. I can organise a date with him if you want.'

'Yeah, right. That's all I need, a charming, over-worked copper looking for a love life.'

'Something bugging you, Brennan? You seem a little edgy this morning.'

'I've got a lot on my mind,' she bit down hard on the end of her pen.

He walked up to her and whispered in her ear, 'I bet you have, darlin'.'

Jill shifted in her seat. Morrissey walked past Chapman's desk on his way out. Chapman was looking at the computer screen, his face twisted in concentration.

'You need more fibre in your diet, son,' Morrissey said.

Chapman removed his glasses and looked up at him.

'The look on your face reminds me of the look my old gran used to get when she was constipated.'

Jill heard Chapman mumble something under his breath.

'It's obvious, isn't it?' Jill said to Morrissey.

'What is?' Morrissey stopped on the threshold, turned around.

'Paloma's and Freddie's deaths. They're related, aren't they?'

'Of course they bloody well are.'

There was an interactive smart board on the far wall. Jill stared across the room at the photos of Paloma and Freddie before her eyes ran along the time lines of what they knew of the last twenty-four hours of their lives. She noticed Chisca's name had been written in a heavy scrawl. 'The common denominator in both cases is Dorin Chisca.'

'You're starting to sound like one of us,' Morrissey laughed and looked across at the board again. 'Don't forget Taggart,' he said. 'The boss reckons he's the second coming of Doctor Jeckyll and Mr Hyde.' Morrissey looked at his watch. 'Well, I'd like to stay and chat, but I'm outta here. Got bad guys to catch.'

Jill turned back to her computer screen.

'Dickhead,' said Chapman.

Brennan knew Morrissey wasn't the most popular detective in the station but he got results.

Choi swivelled around in her seat. 'Don't let him get to you, Matt. Everyone know he's up himself.'

Jill grabbed the bottled water on her desk and unscrewed the lid. She stared into the empty space in front of her and thought about Calida Winfred. What was her part in all this besides painting the innuendos?

'Smile, it can't be all that bad.' Luke walked into the room, cleared a space on his desk and pulled out two sushi rolls and a can of Diet Coke from a plastic bag.

'Luke? What do we know about the fire at Calida Winfred's house? Was it suspicious?'

Jenny turned around on her chair. 'I've been looking at the case notes and she reckons she didn't know what happened that night – had no idea how the fire started. She couldn't even remember how she got out of the house.'

'What did the Arson Squad have to say about it?' Luke popped open the can.

'The damage was so extensive they couldn't pinpoint the exact cause. The house collapsed on itself and because of the number of hot spots, any evidence on how it started was destroyed.'

'Maybe we should take a closer look at Calida Winfred. The fire could have been deliberately lit to scare her off,' Rawlings said. He picked up a marker pen and wrote in bold letters on the whiteboard, *Calida Winfred – fire?* Jill saw him looking at the forensic photos of Freddie and Paloma, just as she had moments before. She wondered if like her, he had noticed the blanks against witnesses, suspects, and forensics.

'What's got me baffled is, if it's the same person responsible for both deaths, why the different MO?' Jill asked.

'You can place too much significance on an MO.' Luke unwrapped his California roll. 'The perp can panic, lose his cool, or the victim's response can change.' He took a bite. A grain of rice fell onto his shirt and he brushed it away. 'Put up too much of a fight and he's forced to use different methods.'

Jill knew he was showing off. The way he was talking, it sounded like he was reciting from a police manual. He had received his detective's designation six months earlier, and whether he meant to or not, he was rubbing her face in the fact. Everyone knew it was only because of the undercover assignment that she was even here at all.

'I forgot to tell you, the boss phoned to say Ted Mackie is driving Calida Winfred down from the Hunter Valley to identify Freddie.' Luke drained the can of Coke and aimed it at the waste paper bin. It landed dead centre. 'Also said for you to find your mate, Taggart, quick smart and bring him in for a chat.'

It was the end of Morrissey's shift and instead of driving straight home he went to Otto's Bar.

He finished what was left of his second beer and decided against another. The last thing he needed was to be pulled over by the local constabulary for D.U.I.

Morrissey was a month away from turning forty-five. He was on his third wife, but this time he knew he'd got it right. Sophie was the perfect fit for him in every way. She didn't complain when he came home late from the pub or was called out to a case in the middle of the night. She was an understanding woman, especially when it came to his job.

Over the years, Morrissey had learnt to compartmentalise the worst of the memories that went with being a police sergeant. He turned them on and off like well-oiled machinery, but after almost four years of trying to forget about Dorin Chisca, the bastard had turned up again like space matter spewed out from a black hole. He knew Chisca's involvement in the Browne and Winfred cases was a problem. He knew what it would mean for him. It was obvious the two deaths were connected, obvious enough; even Jill Brennan had worked it out.

Morrissey knew that in Rimis's mind, Kevin Taggart was a serial killer and Freddie Winfred was his latest victim. He knew Rimis well enough to know he wouldn't give up until he nailed Taggart and had him behind bars. What bothered Col Morrissey was not Rimis's obsession with Taggart, but where the investigation would lead him.

Morrissey's mobile buzzed and he grabbed it from the bar. It was Scott Carver.

'Scotty, how are you cuz? Long time no see.'

'Yeah, I'm fine. Listen Col, I've only got a few minutes, I'm about to go into a meeting. I've been speaking with Mickey Brennan's daughter. She was asking me all sorts of questions. I told her about Dorin Chisca. Told her he was small time but not to be fooled by the fact he didn't have a criminal record.'

'You didn't tell her anything about me, did you?'

'Don't worry, there's no way I'd open my mouth. And Bill Peruzzi isn't going to either.'

'Yeah, I heard about Blinky,' Morrisey said.

Morrissey walked out of Otto's Bar and lit up a cigarette. He threw the empty pack into a garbage bin and walked back to his car. He sat behind the steering wheel and looked out through the windscreen and wondered what he was going to do to get out of the mess he was in. He should have known any offspring of Mickey's would be just like him. Once Mickey Brennan had got a whiff of something rotten, he would never leave it alone.

Chapter Fifteen

'Look who's here, Helen.' The nurse plumped up the pillows and turned down the television.

It had begun slowly at first, a few episodes of forgetfulness, confusion over Christmas and Easter, then the annoying habit of repeating the same stories more than a dozen times. At first Rimis and his brother Peter had thought it was a case of old age catching up with her. Then there were the tests and the diagnosis. Nick knew his mother would have despised the person she'd become.

Helen Rimis was dressed in a pale blue nightdress scattered with sprays of yellow daisies. Nick took her hand and held it in his. 'It's Nicko, Mum.' Nick noticed the bony hand, the finger joints twisted by disease.

'I don't know any Nicko.' Helen Rimis took back her hand. 'Get away from me. I know what you want; it's what you all want. Well, don't think you'll be getting any from me.'

'Mum, it's okay. It me, Nick.' He looked into her eyes and waited for a sign of recognition.

'Nick?'

'Yes, Mum. I've bought you some flowers, roses. They're your favourite.'

The nurse returned to the room with a narrow vase and set it down on the bedside table. Helen Rimis looked at the cream-coloured roses.

'They're lovely.' A smile formed on her thin bluish lips. Her flat chest rose as she took in a sudden breath and he studied her face. Guilt overshadowed him. It hadn't been a conscious decision to stay away; she had just slipped out of his life without him realising it.

'She seems more settled now,' Rimis said to the nurse.

'We don't know where she found the strength to unlock the window. She's as frail as a sparrow. She wasn't in the garden overnight, only an hour or so, since first light when the shift changed. We bought her in and gave her a shower straight away and changed her into a fresh nightdress.'

'Has the doctor been in to see her?' Rimis asked.

'Doctor will be in later today. He might want to change her medication. We've given her a sedative. And we've spoken to maintenance. Someone's coming in later to change the lock on the window –make it harder to open.'

Rimis smiled to put the nurse at ease because she looked embarrassed. Or was it a look of worry he saw on her face? Was she worried that he might report the incident to the Aged Care Complaints Scheme?

Helen Rimis stirred.

'Do you want me to call your brother and tell him what's happened?' The nurse asked.

'No, I'll tell him.' Rimis's shoulders slumped. 'I appreciate what you all do for her, you know.'

The nurse smiled at him before leaving the room.

Helen Rimis loved gardening. Before she became ill and was forced to leave her home in Maroubra, where Rimis now lived, she'd spent almost every day in the garden, tending it. Perhaps that was why she was drawn to the garden outside her window. Some distant memory of better times. She would be disappointed if she saw what Rimis had done, or rather, not done to her garden. It was neglected and overgrown and the roses badly needed pruning. He decided that from now on he would make more of an effort.

Helen Rimis was well cared for at Bayside Nursing Home. It was clean with pleasant surroundings, good food, and friendly, caring staff. Rimis's brother visited every second day for an hour or two; he sat with her, read to her, took her for walks in the garden. Peter Rimis was older than Nick by six years, and over the decades the age gap between them had never closed.

Rimis knew his brother didn't approve of his choice of career or his lifestyle, and he knew Peter thought he should have worked harder on his marriage. If Rimis had, then Fiona would never have left him and he would have had children by now. A few months ago, Peter and his wife Christina tried to fix him up with a nice Greek girl, but they gave up when they realised he was a lost cause.

Without exception, every March for the past five years, Peter and Christina took the boys out of school for a week and headed up the coast to their holiday home at Bluey's Beach, leaving Nick to look after his mother. It was the only thing his brother had ever asked of him. This time was important. It was family time.

Rimis returned to his car and switched on the CD player. By the time he drove into the Station car park, the CD had finished. He glanced at the clock on the dashboard and was surprised it was almost eleven o'clock. Seeing his mother this morning had unnerved him. He wasn't overweight, but he knew he ate lousy food and drank too much. He'd given up the cigarettes more than a year ago. That was something, at least. He knew he had been doing everything wrong and made a mental note to ask Rawlings the name of the gym he belonged to and about the cost of membership. He put on an extra burst of speed and ran up the stairs to his office.

Chapter Sixteen

Rimis sat at his desk and checked his emails. He clicked on a message from Doctor Ross and opened the attachment. It was Paloma Browne's post mortem report. The toxicology and screening results revealed her death had been caused by an overdose of heroin. There were no diatoms found in any of her internal organs or bone marrow, and the blood in her heart had been undiluted, indicating she'd been dead before she entered the river.

Paloma's fingernails hadn't revealed anything; they'd been bitten down to the quick. A nervy type, Rimis thought to himself. No skin fragments were found under them, only a few rayon fibre threads that could have been picked up anywhere.

Brennan stormed into Rimis's office without knocking. She folded her arms against her chest.

'You knew, didn't you?' she said.

'Knew what?'

'Dorin Chisca. He was a suspect in my father's murder enquiry. You knew and you didn't tell me.'

'Close the door and sit down.' He looked at her hands. They were trembling. 'I said, sit down.'

She sat down and he saw her bite her lip.

'Yeah, I knew.'

'Why didn't you tell me?'

'Because I didn't want it to affect the way you dealt with Chisca, or the case. I didn't want you to get all emotional on me and lose perspective.'

'Perspective? Fuck perspective.' She tried to blink the tears away. 'One of the members of the Romanian gang was arrested for what happened that night, but there was talk he was protecting someone, someone higher up the food chain. It was Dorin Chisca, wasn't it?'

'Who've you been talking to?'

'Scott Carver.'

'What the hell are you doing talking to a crime squad commander?'

'He was there the night Dad was killed. I phoned him. I wanted to hear what he had to say about what happened.'

'Did he tell you anything?'

'It was a short phone call. He couldn't tell me a lot because he didn't see it happen, but he did tell me about Chisca.'

'Feel better now you've got that off your chest,' Rimis said.

'Yeah, I do.' She unfolded her arms and sat back in the chair.

'Now you've calmed down, talk to me.'

She took a deep breath and asked him what he knew about her father.

'I knew him only by reputation. You know when one of our own gets killed on the job, there's always a lot of talk. I heard he took a lot of risks. He was hot-headed. Maybe that's where you get it from.'

Brennan looked at him and frowned. 'And Chisca?'

'The drug squad have had their eye on him for four years but he's small time. There are bigger fish to fry. It's all about priorities, budgets, manpower. One thing I did find out, Chisca always seemed to know when we had him under surveillance or if a push was being made to shut him down. No evidence was ever found, or at least, not enough to have him put away.'

Rimis knew Brennan understood what that meant. Chisca had someone in his pocket and it wasn't a for-tune-teller.

'When I first met you, I didn't twig to who you were. That came later when you were assigned to the art fraud case. When we found out Chisca was involved, I didn't know how much you knew about how Mickey died, or even if you wanted to know.'

Brennan squirmed in the chair.

'Look Brennan, I've got Chisca sweating it out in interview room three. If he's got anything to do with your father's death, we'll nail him this time round. I promise you.'

'I want to sit in on the interview.'

'Okay, but pull yourself together. When I call you in, I don't want you saying anything. I want you to watch the body language. I want your impressions.'

'Me?'

'Yes you. Anything wrong with that?'

Dorin Chisca had been alone in the interview room for almost twenty minutes. 'Mr Chisca,' Rimis said as he opened the door. He gave the Romanian one of his stock standard smiles. He sat down across the table from him. 'Can I get you coffee or tea?'

'No, thank you.' Chisca glanced at the audio-visual machine on the table next to him. Rimis followed his eyes.

'We're just having a friendly talk. No need for any of that. Come on, you must be thirsty. Sure I can't get you something? A glass of water maybe?'

Rawlings walked in and sat down next to Rimis.

'No. I am not thirsty. I am in a hurry, and as you know, I am returning to Bucharest at the end of the week. There are many loose ends I need to tie up before I leave.' Chisca flicked his wrist and looked at his chunky, gold watch.

Rimis noticed the tufts of black hair above his knuckles and wondered what the loose ends were and if they had anything to do with Paloma Browne or Freddie Winfred. He pulled a pack of mints out from his shirt pocket and slipped one into his mouth.

'Been in the country long, Dorin?'

'I have resident status. I have been here for ten years.'

'Like living here then?'

'It would be hard not to. Australia is a lucky country. But as I told you yesterday, my parents are elderly. I need to take care of them.'

'Must be hard being an only child. I've got a brother and it helps when you can share the load.' Rimis ignored the surprised look on Rawlings face when he mentioned his family. He kept his gaze steady and studied Chisca's face. It was like interviewing a cut-out character. He looked for something, anything. He was waiting for the cracks to show.

'Did you have anything to do with Freddie Win-fred's murder, Dorin?' Rimis asked in a calm voice.

'What is this?' Chisca slammed a fist on the desk and stood up. 'Of course not. I phoned the emergency number, 000, when I found her. If I killed her, would I have done that? And would I be here now, co-oper-ating with you?'

'Please, sit down. There's no reason to be upset.'

'Upset? I am more than upset, Inspector.'

'Look Dorin, you must appreciate we have ques-tions concerning Miss Winfred's death that we need answered. You must realise, interviewing friends, rel-atives and associates is routine procedure. We need to pursue every lead we can. Now, if you wouldn't mind, please tell me again. What happened? What were you doing at the warehouse?'

Chisca sat at an odd angle in the steeled-framed chair. The chair squeaked.

'I will tell you again. I arrived at the warehouse at ten o'clock. I check the warehouse and storeroom every Monday morning. Always the same time, except for last Monday. I had other things I had to do.'

'Tell me what these things were.'

'The health care in Romania is not as good as it is here. I had a dental appointment. You can check the time.'

'Don't worry. We will. What happened when you turned up at the warehouse?'

'There was this terrible smell, a smell which was very bad. I tried to find out where it was coming from. I walked into the bathroom, I found her there. Found Freddie with her head down the toilet bowl.'

Rimis adjusted his tie and looked around the room. 'Hot in here, isn't it? We've been having a few problems with the air conditioning.' He leaned forward, pinched the bridge of his nose. 'Now, let me get this clear,' he said. 'You check the stock in the warehouse every Monday, but not last Monday.'

'That is what I keep telling you, once a week, every Monday.' Rimis heard the tiredness in Chisca's voice.

'We've been trying to trace Freddie's last movements. The last time anyone saw her was when a black Bentley picked her up from outside her gallery last Sunday week. According to a witness, Freddie was in a big hurry. So, where were you going?' Rimis locked his fingers together and stared into Chisca's dark eyes.

'An investor phoned,' Chisca snapped. 'We went to see him together.'

'What? On a Sunday?'

'Busy, successful people don't always work Monday to Friday, Inspector.'

'Why did you take Freddie with you?' Rimis loosened his tie.

Chisca sighed. 'Freddie Winfred was a charming woman, Inspector. She was very persuasive when it came to dealing with clients, especially male clients. The investor said he could only give us thirty minutes to do the business. He had a plane to catch that afternoon. For some reason, known only to him, he could not wait until he returned.'

'What was this investor's name?'

'Mr Norton, Mr Lionel Norton. He is the Chief Executive Officer of Cairncross Holdings. We went to his office in York Street. I have his secretary's details. She was also working and will confirm the meeting.'

There was a knock on the door. Brennan entered, whispered something in Rimis's ear and walked out again.

'Excuse me for a moment, Dorin.' Rimis and Rawlings stood up.

Chisca shifted in his seat. 'Will we be much longer? I have things I need to do.'

Fifteen minutes later Rimis and Brennan returned to the interview room. Rimis knew from experience that enough time had passed for Chisca to be wondering what had been important enough for him to leave part way through the interview. It was a tactic Rimis often used to make a suspect nervous.

Rimis slapped a file on the desk and sat down. He brushed away an imagined speck of fluff from his shirt before he opened the file and picked up a crime scene photo of Paloma Browne. He pushed it across the table towards Chisca.

'Have you ever seen this young woman before?'

Chisca leant forward, tilted his head to one side. His face showed no emotion. 'How can I tell? Part of her face is missing.' He sat back in his chair with a blank look on his face.

Rimis pointed to the photo of her left wrist; it clearly showed a butterfly tattoo. 'Know anyone with a tattoo like that?'

Chisca shook his head.

'Well, take a look at this then.' Rimis produced another photo from the file and pushed it across the table. 'It's a photo of the same girl at her year twelve formal.'

'I do not know her. I have never seen her before.'

Rimis took the photo back and looked at it. This was what Paloma Browne had looked like before she was murdered. Intelligent eyes, tumbling long red hair. 'Her name was Paloma Browne,' Rimis said. 'She was a twenty-year-old art student. She died from an overdose of heroin. Then she was put into an industrial garbage bag liner and dumped in the tidal section of the Lane Cove River.' Rimis drummed his fingernails on the desk, leant forward and looked into Chisca's eyes. 'She was Freddie's gallery assistant. Freddie ever mention her? Paloma. An unusual name, don't you think? Not a name you'd forget in a hurry.'

'I told you at the warehouse when you asked me the same question, I do not know this girl.'

Rimis held up the photo again. 'Sure you don't know her?'

'How many times do I have to tell you?'

Rimis shoved another photo in front of Chisca. 'And this woman, do you recognise her?'

'Do not be ridiculous, Inspector. Of course I do. It is Freddie.'

'Not a good way to die, you'd have to agree?' Rimis asked.

Chisca shook his head a number of times.

Rimis returned the photos to the file and closed it. 'Seems strange you didn't know Paloma Browne.'

'I do not know what more you want me to tell you. I have told you everything I know. I did not know the young woman and I did not kill her, or Freddie. You cannot pin these murders on me.'

Rimis looked at Brennan. 'Did you hear that, Senior? I don't recall asking Mr Chisca if he murdered that poor girl. He's only here because we wanted to talk to him about Freddie.'

Chisca's eyes flashed in anger. He stood up and thumped his fist on the table. 'If you wish to continue this senseless questioning, I would like my solicitor present. I know my rights.'

'Of course you know your rights and you're entitled to have your legal representative present if you want to be formal about all this, but I thought you just dropped in for a quiet chat to help us with our enquiries.'

'Is this what we are having Inspector? A quiet chat?' Chisca looked at the audiovisual recorder again.

'Thank you for coming in, Mr Chisca. We have your signed statement, but we may need to speak to you again.'

Chisca pushed the chair out of his way and walked towards the door. 'So that is it then?' he asked.

'Yes, at least for now. And Mr Chisca, it might be an idea to cancel your flight back to Romania, at least until this is sorted. Hope you took out flight cancellation insurance.'

Chapter Seventeen

Rimis looked at Brennan sitting across the desk from him. 'Give me your thoughts on Chisca. You believe him?'

'I think I do. I've checked his story about rushing off with Freddie to see a client. Norton's PA confirmed the meeting. The dental appointment checked out too. But I don't believe him when he said he didn't know Paloma.'

'What about the warehouse. Anyone see or hear anything?'

'It was a Sunday, nobody was working.'

'No chance of a CCTV, I suppose?'

'It's only a small estate. There's no security.'

'What about Nicolae Vladu? Anybody know where he was while all this was happening?' Rimis asked.

'The Sarge's got Luke looking into his whereabouts,' she said.

'Paloma Browne's post mortem report doesn't say anything about needle track marks, so we can assume she wasn't a regular user,' Rimis said.

'What about the severed arm?'

'A clean amputation, consistent with a sharp object. Doctor Ross made it clear in her report that interpretation was difficult. Lane Cove River is a busy water-way, plenty of water-skiers, power boats and ferries about; a propeller blade could have caused the amputation. Could also explain the trauma to the face.'

'You know what I'm thinking?'

'No, Brennan. I never know what you're thinking. You're a complete mystery to me.'

She smiled. 'Maybe someone had a grudge against her. An ex-druggie boyfriend who didn't like the fact she was clean and had plans for her life.'

'Anything better than that?' Rimis sat back in his chair.

'Choi and I spoke to the parents. The father wasn't on speaking terms with her and didn't know the mother was seeing her. Mrs Browne had a phone call the day before Paloma went missing. Paloma was excited about something and wanted to meet her for coffee to tell her all about it.'

'Did you ask her if she knew why she was so excited?'

'She didn't know what it was about, all she said was that she sounded happier than she had for a long time.'

'So what happened?'

'Paloma never showed. When the mother tried to contact her and couldn't track her down, she reported her missing. When I asked her about drugs, she told me she was definitely clean. She was working hard at the gallery and at college and was saving to go to some fancy art school in Paris.'

'What about the studio?' Rimis frowned.

'She was dossing there. A mattress on the floor and

a makeshift kitchen. She had photocopies of Brett Whiteley prints pinned on all the walls and cardboard boxes of art books.'

'That would be right. I heard he was her pin-up boy,' Rimis said.

'We've got someone from IT going through the files and emails on her laptop. It's speculation, but let's assume she found out the innuendos she was painting were a front for the drugs? Remember the note I found in Freddie's office? *I know what you're both up to and it's going to cost.* She'd already resigned from the gallery and was excited about something, excited enough to want to tell her mum about it. She could have already had the money for her air fare.'

'Well if she did, what did she do with it? There's no evidence she bought a ticket, no transactions on her debit or credit cards, or withdrawals from her bank accounts. Unless she paid for it in cash.' Rimis said. He stood up from his desk. 'Might be an idea to check the airlines.'

There was a knock on the door. Rawlings walked in. 'We've just had a result from Crime Stoppers, boss. A bus driver saw Paloma, or someone fitting her description, around eight-thirty the night she died. She got off his bus in Oxford Street, outside a travel agency. Choi and I are going to pay the agency a visit. She would have passed by there on her way to the gallery. Someone might have been working late. There was another sighting around nine o'clock. She was walking along Queen Street, looking in shop windows.'

'I left the Dunworth around nine that night,' Brennan said. 'Kevin left at least five minutes before me.'

'So we can place Taggart at the scene. The timing is certainly right. What happened after you left the Gallery? Did you see him again?'

'No, I didn't. I walked straight back to my car. There was a car parked in front of my mine. It pulled away from the kerb when I walked into James Street, but I didn't have any reason to take notice of who was driving, or if they had a passenger. I wish I had.'

Rimis opened the top drawer of his desk and swept in a pile of papers. 'Let me know if you find out anything from the travel agent, Rawlings.' Rimis looked at his watch. 'Grab your bag, Brennan, we're going to Freddie's apartment. I've managed to get Forensics. They should be there by now. Then we'll go and pay Scott Carver a visit and find out how we're going to handle Dorin Chisca.'

All the rooms in Freddie's apartment were sealed. The UV lights were set up and the surfaces were being dusted. Rimis nodded to the officer at the door and he and Brennan signed the attendance sheet. Brennan pulled out her notebook and a pen and leafed through the pages. Rimis asked her how she had accessed the apartment. When she told him the door wasn't locked, he raised his eyebrows and left it at that.

Brennan walked behind Rimis into the apartment, but turned around when she heard a woman's voice calling out.

'Excuse me, Kylie.' It was the woman from across the hall. She was standing in her doorway.

'What should I do with it?' The woman asked.

Brennan gave her a blank look, tucked her hair behind her ear and walked back out into the hall.

'Your aunt's kaftan. What should I do with it now she won't be wearing it again?'

'I'm sure she would want you to have it,' Brennan said.

'I don't want it. It's bad luck to wear a dead person's clothes.' She stepped back inside her apartment. A moment later, she was in the hall again and pressed the kaftan into Brennan's arms. 'Here, take it. You're family; it's right you should have it.'

Brennan was about to say something, but before she had a chance, the woman closed the door in her face.

Rimis looked amused. She walked past him and into Freddie's bedroom and tossed the kaftan on the bed.

'So, it's Auntie Freddie now, is it Kylie?' Rimis grinned. Brennan rolled her eyes. They walked into the lounge room and looked out at the view across the balcony.

'Nothing much to go on, is there?'

'You're a mind-reader Brennan.'

Chapter Eighteen

Area Commander Scott Carver's office was spacious and well-appointed, as one would expect of a high-ranking officer. Behind his desk was a bookcase of technical and procedural manuals. On his desk were a lap top computer and a few open files. Rimis and Jill had been in his office for less than fifteen minutes when they stood to leave.

'Could I have a word, Sir?' Jill asked. She looked at Rimis. 'In private?'

'I'll be waiting in the car,' Rimis said, before he closed the door behind him.

'You can dispense with the Sir business now. Rimis has gone.'

Jill sat down again. 'I had no idea you were an area commander when I met you at Bea and Harry's. And I didn't recognise your voice either when I spoke to you on the phone. Some detective I'm going to make.'

Scott Carver laughed and sat back in his chair. 'If it's any consolation, I didn't recognise your voice either.'

'This is embarrassing.' Jill tucked a stray hair behind her ear. 'Bea should have told me who you were. And if you don't mind me asking, what were you doing at Bea and Harry's anyway? It didn't seem like your scene, you know, babies and everything.'

'I didn't want to miss the chance to meet you. Bea and Harry told me we had a lot in common. I didn't realise how much, until today.'

'I was at an unfair advantage then,' she smiled and crossed her legs. 'You're probably wondering what I want to talk to you about.'

This was awkward. What was she doing here? The way he was looking at her now, she sensed he felt sorry for her. She was grateful when he put her out of her misery.

'If I was a betting man, I'd say it had something to do with Dorin Chisca and your father.' Scott Carver moved around from behind his desk and sat down next to her. 'What do you want to know? I've already told you I wasn't with your father when he was shot.'

Jill leant forward. 'Chisca claims he wasn't there that night at Lakemba, and I know there's no evidence to suggest he was. But I've got a feeling he knows who shot my father and why.'

'I can't tell you much more than you already know. You must have read the reports.'

'Yeah, I read them. It's just I want to find some answers but I don't know what questions I should be asking.'

'Look, I'm sorry, I can't tell you what you want to hear. There was no evidence that Chisca had anything to do with Mickey's death.'

Jill nodded.

'Did you know him well? My father, I mean.'

'Mickey was a good officer. Just keep that in mind

if you speak to Chisca, or anyone else. Don't be too quick to believe what people might want to tell you.' Carver stood up, smiled. 'Jill, I was wondering. Tyrone Maitland is having an exhibition at the Harvey Street Gallery this weekend. We could have lunch afterwards if...'

'Sorry, Scott, but I've got this rule that I don't date cops. And, I've got my Bull Ring coming up. I need to stay focused. There's a lot happening in my life right now.' Jill held out her hand to him to shake it, and he took it gently and rubbed her wrist with his thumb. She realised she had got nowhere apart from being asked out on a date. Another dead end.

Jill walked out of Parramatta Police HQ and headed towards the car park. The worst of the day's heat was trapped beneath the footpath. It was always a few degrees warmer out west and her shirt was sticking to her back like an army of sucking leeches. She grabbed a small pot of lip-gloss from her bag, smoothed the greasy mix over her lips and tasted strawberries. What she would do for a cool drink and a swim right now.

By the time she got back to the car, perspiration was running down her neck. Rimis was sitting in the passenger seat, listening to the radio. The engine was running and the air con was on.

'So what was all that about?' Rimis asked.

'Just wanted to talk to him about Dad.'

On the drive back to the city she felt cool enough

to be able to think clearly about what had just happened. Scott Carver, Harry's friend, not a gynaecologist, a Police Commander. *Shit*. She was definitely going to kill Bea now.

Chapter Nineteen

Kevin examined the welts on his face in the bath-room mirror then ran the cold water tap. He shuddered, sensed his mother's presence. Even in death, she still had power over him. Whenever he thought about her, his skin began to itch and realised there was no escaping her.

He never told anybody about the punishments; thought nobody would have believed him. If his mis-demeanours had been judged major, she would pun-ish him by sending him to stand in the toilet bowl. She would then walk into the bathroom and empty her bladder. He dismissed the image and looked at his hair. It needed combing and he could do with a shave.

He patted his face with a towel, threw the towel on the floor and walked into the bedroom. A sports bag lay open on the bare, saggy mattress. It was packed with his only possessions: a threadbare bible, his moth-er's battered leather diary, a few changes of underwear, clean shirts, a pair of denim jeans that he had recently bought, and a waterproof bag for his toiletries. He was upset about leaving the apartment and the com-fortable life he had made for himself, but he had no choice. He knew if Inspector Rimis hadn't already fit-ted the pieces of the puzzle together, it wouldn't be long before he did. He hadn't left the apartment for days; now was the time to make his move. He had his sights set on another victim. This time it would be the last and he felt better knowing that. 'Set thine house in order,' he mumbled to himself.

He opened the top drawer of his bedside table and took out a small metal paint box, an ordinary kitchen teaspoon, a plastic straw, and an expired gym membership card. He recognised the irony of using the card.

He removed the lid from the paint box and scooped out a generous amount of the white powder he had taken from the frame of *North Coast Summers*. His hand trembled. He chopped the cocaine into neat thick lines, the way he had seen it done on *You Tube*. He closed his right nostril with his index finger. He snorted one of the lines. The sudden rush surprised him. The sensation spread across his soft palate. For good measure, he gulped down a handful of the little white pills Nicolae Vladu had given him. With the surge of adrenalin running through his veins, he felt he could take on anybody.

He left the apartment with *North Coast Summer*s under his arm and threw the set of keys into the bushes near the bank of letterboxes by the entrance. He crossed Cleveland Street against the traffic lights and looked over his shoulder to make sure he wasn't being followed before he turned left and walked a few blocks towards the city. A police car drove slowly past and he pulled his baseball cap down low over his eyes. Head down, he continued walking through the quiet leafy streets to where he had parked his car. He opened the boot and put the painting and his bag inside. His heart was racing. He scratched his chest through his shirt then wrapped his hand around the object in his trouser pocket. When a taxi picked him up a few streets later, he slunk down low in the back seat and thought about how easy it would be this time.

Chapter Twenty

The reception area at Chatswood Police Station was quiet. The duty sergeant was standing behind the desk, shuffling a pile of papers. Ted Mackie was by Calida's side on a timber bench reading a brochure on keeping kids safe. He had dispensed with his usual Hawaiian shirt and was wearing a white linen collared shirt and a pair of fashionable denim jeans. When Rimis appeared, Ted put aside the brochure and got to his feet. Calida stood and walked over to him. 'I've just come back from the morgue, Inspector.'

Rimis had been present enough times when relatives were making a formal identification to know what Calida had just been through. It was something nobody should ever have to experience.

'Come upstairs to my office, we can talk better there.'

'I know this is a difficult time for you Cal, especially with the story in the papers.' Rimis massaged the back of his neck and avoided looking at her.

'Why haven't you found Freddie's killer?' The skin around her eyes crinkled into deep lines.

'We're doing everything we can.' Rimis was surprised by her abruptness and was angry because he had nothing to tell her. He flipped opened the file on his desk and picked out three photos. Kevin Taggart, Nicolae Vladu, Dorin Chisca.

'Do you recognise any of these men?' Rimis lined the photos up in front of her. 'Take your time, have a good look.'

Calida slipped her hands into her bag and pulled out her reading glasses. She studied the photos, swallowed hard and handed them back to him.

'I've never seen any of these men before.'

Rimis reached for another file. 'What about this one?' Rimis produced a photo of Paloma Browne at her year twelve formal.

'Paloma Browne. She certainly was an attractive girl. Freddie hired her after I left the gallery. Her photo and details of her death were on the front page of all the papers. Do you think whoever killed Freddie, killed Paloma?'

'We're not sure at this stage,' he said. 'Tell me about Paloma and Freddie. What sort of relationship did they have? Did they get on?'

'I think they did. At least as far as I know. Freddie was a hard taskmaster but she was always fair. Paloma was a wild girl; Freddie took pity on her and gave her a job. Freddie told me she was saving up to study at the Sorbonne.'

'Did you know she painted Whiteleys for Freddie?'

'Freddie never said, but I had my suspicions. She knew I didn't like Whiteley's work. I think it's vulgar, so when she insisted I try my hand at them, I assumed Paloma had saved enough money for her airfare to Paris and Freddie wanted me to take over from her to fill the gap.'

'We know from an email Paloma sent Freddie that she'd resigned from the gallery, so you could be right,' Rimis said. 'I want you to take a look at these. We have the originals downstairs in the lockup, but I thought you might be able to tell from the photos.'

Calida stared at the coloured photos and studied each one carefully. Some she held up to the light, others she picked up then placed to one side. She removed her glasses. 'I painted all of them, except for the Whiteleys. Paloma would have painted them. She followed Brett's style closely, much better than I could have.' Calida looked at Rimis and frowned. 'So, what's all this got to do with Freddie's murder?'

'We found forged provenance certificates in the safe at the gallery. We believe Freddie was involved in a money laundering scheme, as well as art fraud.'

'You're crazy. Freddie? Art fraud perhaps, but money laundering?'

'Art lends itself to it.' Rimis knew money-laundering was simple. 'When someone has illegal money they want to get rid of, it has to look like it came from legitimate sources. I know it must be hard for you to accept, but we've found receipts for art purchases that don't match their true value. We believe Freddie may have been selling your innuendos and genuine works for cash as a way to launder money earned through illegal drug trafficking. She'd resell the paintings and —'

Calida got to her feet, visibly upset. 'Freddie was my sister, Inspector. I won't sit here and listen to her good name being bandied around like this.'

Ted drove back through the cross-city tunnel to the eastern suburbs and dropped Calida outside the gallery. 'Are you sure you'll be all right? I could stay with you, or come back in an hour and drive you to Freddie's apartment.'

'I'm okay, Ted, really. After I've finished here, I'll get a taxi to Freddie's. It's not far.'

'Well, if you're sure.'

Calida watched Ted drive away. She unlocked the gallery's front door and walked down the hall to Freddie's office. She was surprised. Apart from the messy desk, the office had changed little since she was here last. She hadn't stepped inside the gallery since before the fire. What would she would do with the gallery now Freddie was dead?

She sat down in the plush red chair behind the antique desk and looked at the blank computer screen. She wasn't sure what she was looking for or what she expected to find. Inspector Rimis had told her the police had removed Freddie's paper records and downloaded her computer files. She wondered if Freddie had changed the computer password and was about to enter *sisters* in the log in command box when she heard the click of the front door and the shifting of feet on the timber floorboards outside the office.

'Ted, is that you?' There was no answer. 'Ted?' She tried to remember if she had locked the front door when she came in.

'It's you,' she said. She got to her feet.

'Yes, it is me, Calida. It has been a long time.'

Vladu followed in behind Chisca and stood in one corner of the room.

'I see you brought your shadow with you.' She nodded towards Vladu. He showed no sign of emotion or acknowledgement. 'How dare you come in here like this and frighten me half to death?'

Chisca sat down in a chair across the desk from her and removed a single cigarette from a silver case. He lit up.

'Do you have to smoke? It's such a filthy habit.'

Chisca drew in a lung-full of nicotine and crossed his legs. 'Sit down Calida, no need to stand on my account.' He blew a ring of smoke towards her.

'What do you want?' Calida sat down. 'You've already taken everything that was important to me: my sister, my home, my career.' She knew Dorin Chisca was a violent, unpredictable man, but whatever he wanted from her, she knew she wasn't going to make the same mistake twice. She would face him head on and not scamper away like she did the last time she came up against him.

'Your sister was trying to double cross me.'

'What are you talking about?'

'She was trying to outsmart me. She had you paint an innuendo of *North Coast Summers* and then she substituted it for the original. She was going to resell it, take from me what was rightfully mine.'

'Impossible. Freddie wouldn't do such of thing. She asked me to paint her a copy because it had been sold. It was a painting she admired; she was disappointed she hadn't bought it. And let's get things quite clear from the start. I had no idea she'd taken up with you after the fire. The fire you started.'

'That was just a little misunderstanding.'

'It was a warning. And it worked, didn't it? I signed over the business to Freddie and left Sydney for good. Far away from all your dirty secrets.'

Calida pulled open the top drawer of the desk. Vladu reached inside his coat pocket but dropped his hands to his side when she pulled out a tall bottle of whiskey and two glass tumblers. She thumped them down on the desk in front of her. Freddie always liked to keep the whiskey in her desk drawer in case of emergencies. Calida regarded this an emergency.

'Want a drink?'

Chisca nodded and uncrossed his legs in a feminine way.

She poured out a generous amount of whiskey and handed him a glass. She poured a drink for herself, swirled the whiskey around, tossed her head back and gulped it down in one mouthful. She poured herself another and leant back and closed her eyes for a moment. When she opened them again she stared at him.

'So, when did you get Freddie involved? You said you would kill her if I ever told her what was going on between the two of us, or if I went to the police about the forgeries, the drugs, or the fire. I kept my side of the bargain. What about you, Dorin?' She slammed her glass down on the desk. 'Was it you? Did you kill her?' Calida was on her feet now. Her head was spinning from the emotion and from the whiskey.

'Of course not, it is not my style. You insult me by even accusing me of such a thing.' Chisca leant forward and flicked cigarette ash onto the desk.

'Well, who did then? Was it you?' she said to Vladu.

154

Vladu took a step forward. Chisca waved him back.

'No, it wasn't Nicolae. I have no idea who killed Freddie.'

'Why are you here then? What do you want from me? The police think Freddie was involved in money laundering. Is this what all this is about?'

'No, I am here for the watercolour. I paid Kevin Taggart good money for *North Coast Summers*. I could have simply taken it, but it was meant as a gift for my parents. The gift would have been insincere if I had stolen it from him.' Chisca drained his glass and helped himself to more whiskey. 'Someone has cheated me, Calida. I cannot say who it was. Perhaps it was Freddie, or Kevin Taggart himself. The frame was filled with a kilo of cocaine. Someone took the original from the storeroom in my warehouse and replaced it with your innuendo.

'I would like to compliment you, by the way. It was very good. It had me fooled until I picked it up and looked closely at the signature. It was not right. You really should take more care with your signatures.' Chisca slammed his glass on the desk and the contents spilled. His face darkened.

'Where is it? Where's the original? I have had enough of playing these games.'

Calida sat rigid in her chair and avoided his wild, dark eyes. 'I don't know where it is. Freddie didn't tell me anything about what happened to the innuendos after I painted them, and I never asked.'

Chisca glared at her. 'I hope you are telling me the truth, Calida, because Vladu is going to pay a call on Mr Taggart. If he does not find the painting, he will come back here to tear this place apart and while he is at it, he might just do the same to you.'

The lock mechanism was simple. Vladu leaned up against the door, listened for the click and pushed it open with his shoulder. He stood in the middle of Kevin's empty apartment and looked about him. The blood drained from his face. He wasn't expecting this. He wasn't used to this kind of evil. He was here to find the watercolour and return it to its rightful owner. The women's faces were pinched, shrivelled, bloodless. Red, swollen eyes followed him around the room. He stopped to look at each individual painting. The same woman, with different feverish expressions. Every canvas had one thing in common: words painted across the face. *For the wages of sin is death.*

Vladu didn't have much time, he knew the sooner he was out of here the better. In the bedroom he searched under the bed, ran his hand under the mattress. He found nothing. He opened the wardrobe and came face to face with its emptiness. The wire clothes hangers were all bare. In the bathroom, he pushed the shower curtain to one side. Nothing.

He dialled Chisca's number. 'There is nothing here, Sef,' he said, using the Romanian word for boss.

'What, no painting?'

'I have bad feeling about this guy. I think he is one sick bastard. He is gone, taken everything with him. No clothes, nothing.'

'Nothing at all?'

'There are some paintings here, but they are not worth bothering with. What is it you want me to do?'

Chapter Twenty-One

Calida unlocked the front door to Freddie's apartment with the keys Rimis had handed back to her after Forensics had finished. She walked around the apartment searching for the watercolour even though she was convinced it wasn't here. When she walked into Freddie's bedroom, she saw a kaftan lying across the bed. She picked it up and hoped to smell some trace of Freddie on it, but there was none. She collapsed onto the bed and thought of what Dorin Chisca was going to do to her if he didn't find the painting. She should have told Freddie about the Romanian. If she had, she would have known to avoid him. She was a fool to think he wouldn't prey on her sister like he had on her.

The next morning, Cal woke with a start. Sleep had come to her, two hours before sunrise. She changed out of her clothes and dragged Freddie's kaftan over her head. She looked in the full-length mirror and was surprised by what she saw. The kaftan was cool and comfortable.

In the bathroom she threw handfuls of cold water on her face. She was frightened when she saw the image in the mirror looking back at her. She found herself thinking of Ted and hoped he would understand what she was about to do.

Halfway down Liverpool Street, she walked past a Vietnamese bakery with its tantalising smells of freshly baked bread and pastries. But she knew there would be plenty of time afterwards to eat. She walked to Town Hall station and struggled with the steep stairs down to the North Shore Line platform. It was only a few minutes until the next train to Chatswood was due to arrive.

Rimis and Brennan were about to take the stairs down to the canteen when Jenny Choi came up behind them.

'Boss.'

Rimis turned around. 'What is it?'

'We have a development.'

'Don't talk in riddles, Choi.'

'Calida Winfred is downstairs in interview room two. She wants to speak to you. Says she's come to confess to the murders of her sister and Paloma Browne.'

'Christ. You better bring her up to my office. Is she on her own?'

'Yeah.'

Calida walked into Rimis's office with Choi at her side. Brennan and Rimis got to their feet.

'What's all this about a confession, Cal? Come in and sit down.' Rimis was surprised to see her wearing one of her sister's kaftans. The colour suited her, but it was two sizes too large for her small frame.

'Has anyone offered you something to drink?' Brennan asked.

'No, they haven't dear, but I don't want anything.'

Rimis pulled a chair out and Calida sat down.

'It's all my fault, Inspector.' Her hands were trembling. 'Why didn't I just open my stupid mouth and tell her? If I had, she would still be alive, and so would that poor girl. If I had come to you after the fire and not run off with my tail between my legs, Dorin Chisca would be behind bars now and none of this would have happened.'

'Hold on, Cal. What's this all about?'

Calida's face crumpled. The full force of her grief filled the room. 'By remaining silent I might as well have killed them both with my own two hands.'

Rimis was relieved. He realised what she was telling him. 'Don't be so hard on yourself,' he said. 'None of this is your fault.' He handed her a clean handkerchief from his pocket. 'Take your time and, when you're ready, you can tell me everything.'

'It all started with that awful man,' she said as she dabbed at her eyes. Rimis grabbed a chair and sat down next to her.

'I wasn't completely honest with you when you showed me the photos. One of the men was Dorin Chisca, the other was Nicolae Vladu, his assistant. I met Dorin about twelve months ago. He came into the gallery and we struck up a conversation. We talked about the Heidelberg School and I told him I was an artist and painted in their style. At the time, the Gallery was struggling. I was trying to make ends meet.'

'Go on.'

'Dorin is a charming, good-looking man. I can't tell you how many years it had been since a man paid me as much attention as he did that day. We talked for some time and over lunch he told me he wanted to get into the decorative art business. He said there was a market for innuendos of Heidelberg and contemporary Australian artists among investors and collectors. I couldn't see any harm in it and he assured me he would be only selling the art to friends and business acquaintances. There was never any hint of passing them off as originals.'

'So you went ahead with it.'

'Of course I did. Why wouldn't I?' She wiped her nose on Rimis's handkerchief. 'I would have been mad not to. Dorin paid me well and he made me feel as if I was painting to please him. I decided to keep what I was doing from Freddie, not because I thought there was anything wrong with it, but because of the money. I loved my sister dearly Inspector, but she was an extravagant type of person. She was drawn to the dollar.'

'Did Freddie know what was going on between you and Chisca?'

'No, not as far as I know. He collected the paintings from the gallery and paid me in cash on Freddie's day off. One day, a painting was left behind. I ran out onto the street to flag him down, but I was too late – he was already pulling away, but I saw the name on the side of the van. Chisca Plumbing Supplies. I found the address in the phone directory and drove to his warehouse. I was surprised by how little stock there was; only a few aisles of toilets, wash basins. You know, the usual plumbing fittings. It was only afterwards I realised what was really going on.'

'And what was going on?' Rimis asked.

She leaned towards him and whispered, 'Drugs, Inspector. Drugs.'

Chapter Twenty-Two

Rimis marched into the Major Incident Room. 'I want everyone in here for a briefing in five minutes, and I mean five minutes.' He stepped out of the way of two uniformed officers carrying dusty archive boxes into the room, then walked back down the corridor to his office.

Brennan got up from her desk and took the stairs down to the canteen to tell Jenny and Matt to get back upstairs. The boss was on a rampage.

Less than five minutes later, Rimis was back in the Incident Room. He looked at the uniformed officers and the detectives who had been assigned to the Winfred and Browne cases. The Super had managed to borrow four DCs from Gladesville LAC, but it wasn't a big team, nowhere big enough for the investigation into two homicides everyone knew were linked. Serious faces looked back at him. A few of the officers were drinking coffee from take-away cups; others had a look about them that said they'd seen and heard it all before.

'Alright boys and girls, listen up,' Rimis said. 'I'll dispense with the pleasantries and get right to it. Freddie Winfred's PM results are in.' He passed copies of the report to Matt Chapman and he handed them out. 'The report confirms it: blunt force trauma. She was still alive when her head hit the toilet bowl in Chisca's warehouse. She may have lost consciousness soon afterwards. After the toilet bowl was filled with water from a bucket, a towel was lodged in the neck of the bowl and her head was rammed into it. Whoever did this to her, was strong enough to hold her down until she drowned. There's a whole lot of anger and rage here. We've got blood samples from the scene, but there are no matching results so far.'

'What about Freddie's apartment, Boss?' Rawlings asked.

'Forensics didn't find anything significant, just a few finger prints which we're in the process of eliminating.' Rimis looked at Brennan standing at the back of the room.

'We've ruled Dorin Chisca out. He's got an alibi for the time of both murders. Both as tight as a duck's proverbial. I've got a gut feeling Taggart's involved somehow, so I've decided to re-visit the deaths of Nora Taggart and Edi and Rhoda Blake. Choi, I want you on this. Come and see me in my office after we've finished here.' Choi nodded and scribbled in her notebook.

'In case some of you haven't done your homework, neither Edi, Rhoda Blake or Nora Taggart's deaths were considered suspicious; natural causes in the case of Nora, accidental with the Blakes. Worth noting, though, all three women had two things in common; their association with Kevin Taggart and the day of the week they died. Sunday. As most of you are aware,

I've had my suspicions about Taggart's involvement in the Blake sisters' deaths.

'Brennan tells me Taggart had an unhealthy fascination for Freddie Winfred, so if she stuffed up or did something to disappoint him, he may have retaliated. At least it won't hurt to start with him, ask him a few questions.' Rimis looked out at the sea of faces and cleared his throat.

'Folks, Taggart's life story isn't one you want to be reading to your kiddies at bedtime. His father died in a car accident on Taggart's fifth birthday. The mother blamed him. Worth noting, Nora Taggart was never in the running for Australian Mum of the Year. She was a neurotic alcoholic who seemed to enjoy punishing and humiliating Kevin whenever he displeased her. This is the only useful link we have to Freddie's death. If I'm right about Taggart, he committed these murders on a Sunday based on his childhood experiences.'

'Do we know what day Paloma was murdered boss?' Choi asked.

'Friday, so the pattern doesn't fit. I don't believe he had anything to do with her death. Drugs and young girls aren't Taggart's thing.'

'Do we know where Taggart is now?' Rawlings asked.

'Brennan tells me he's gone to ground. It's important we find him before he does any more damage. Don't be fooled by this guy, he's a creepy little bastard. Just because he looks ordinary, don't underestimate him. Chapman, I want an APB out on him. I want every point of departure alerted: trains, airports, buses, and highway patrols. Brennan, I want you and Rawlings to go around to his apartment, check with his neighbours again to see if they've seen him. Anybody have anything to add?'

Chapter Twenty-Three

There was a knock at the door. Morrissey slouched into Rimis's office and took a seat across from him. 'Heard about Chisca. Good result.'

'Yeah.' Rimis looked up from his crossword puzzle. 'He's been charged with supply and dealing. He's in remand waiting bail application.'

'Was he importing?'

'No, strictly wholesale. Even so, he's looking at a hefty sentence and it doesn't look like he'll be visiting his folks back home any time soon. He had a network of buyers around the country and a system of codes. Depending on what artist you bought, you got amphetamines, cannabis, or cocaine.' Rimis drained his coffee cup. 'He was clever, I'll give him that. When the Drug Squad removed the frames from the paintings in his warehouse storeroom, they found heroin with a street value of around two hundred and eighty grand. They also found cash in his apartment, along with some jewellery.'

'Selling up before heading back home,' Morrissey said. 'So what's happening with the Paloma Browne case?' He sat back in his chair and crossed his legs.

'Still ours, but not much to go on. Chisca's got an

alibi for the night she was murdered; he was at a trivia night, at least twenty people at the Great Northern Hotel can vouch for him.'

'What about Vladu?' Morrissey asked.

'Gone back to the motherland, skipped before we had a chance to ask him any questions. He has disappeared for now, but he'll turn up. Chisca's parents have moved from their run-down flat in a tower block in Pitesti to a modern nursing home in Constanta. I've got a feeling Vladu was acting on instructions. He murders Paloma, skips the country, takes care of Chisca's parents for him, and holds onto what's left of the money.'

Rimis's mobile phone rang. He checked the caller ID. He decided not to answer it. 'Thought you'd want to know, I had a visit from Calida Winfred. She blames herself for what happened to Freddie and Paloma.'

Morrissey looked surprised. He pulled out a pack of cigarettes and a lighter.

'Put them away, Col.'

Morrissey shrugged and returned the cigarettes and lighter to his pocket.

'She was involved with Chisca from the start. When she found out he was using her innuendos to traffic drugs, she threatened him with going to the police. Before she had a chance to do or say anything, he set fire to her house. It did the trick, scared her off and she kept her mouth shut.'

'So the old girl didn't suspect the innuendos she painted for Freddie had something to do with Chisca?' Morrissey asked.

'She thought he'd moved on to bigger and better

things. Calida had no idea Freddie was involved with him.'

Morrissey shook his head.

'Listen, I need to talk to you, Col. People are beginning to notice.'

'Notice what?'

'Your attitude.' Rimis gave him a frosty look.

'It's Chapman isn't it? He's a fucking girl. I just had a bit of a joke with him.'

'It's not only Chapman.' Rimis sat back in his chair. 'Everyone's sick of your outbursts, and your crude jokes. And you stink of ciggies and booze.'

'Jesus Christ, Nick, nag, nag, nag. You sound like Sophie when I've forgotten to take out the wheelie bin.'

Rimis leaned forward over his desk. 'I don't know what your problem is but you better pull yourself together or the complaints are going to become official.'

Morrissey stared angrily at Rimis. 'And I suppose you agree with them?' Morrissey stood up to leave.

'I'm just warning you, that's all. As your boss and as a friend.'

Morrissey's phone rang. He stood up and took it from his hip pocket and looked at the screen. He was about to answer it, when he saw the look on Rimis's face.

'There's something else I want to talk to you about. Sit down.'

'Well what is it?'

'Mickey Brennan,' Rimis said. 'You were with him the night he got shot. I've been looking through the case notes and there are a few things that don't add up about that night. I thought you might be able to shed some light.'

'It was four years ago Nick, the memory's not what it was. Look I have to take this call.'

'Try,' Rimis insisted.

Morrissey pressed the decline button on his phone and put it back in his pocket. He sat down.

'Look, the scum who went down for Brennan's murder were all Romanian,' Rimis said. 'The guy who pulled the trigger had an IQ with a minus sign in front of it, so I can't see him being the guy in charge. There were mumblings at the time that there was someone in the background, pulling the strings. Dorin Chisca's name popped up. What do you remember about that night? It would mean a lot to Brennan if we could lay some ghosts to rest.'

Morrissey shifted in his chair, stood up and closed the door. He walked back to Rimis's desk. His face was flushed. 'All I can tell you is, at the time, there was a spate of home invasions in Lakemba. There was talk Romanian drug dealers from Melbourne had come into the area and were trying to muscle in on the local Middle Eastern gangs. They were linked to all sorts of things, not just drugs but social security fraud and extortion. Brennan, Carver, Peruzzi and I were assigned to the case. We had an anonymous tip off, something was going down that night.'

'Go on,' Rimis said.

'We turned up at this address in Wattle Street. It was late, almost midnight. The street was quiet, no traffic, not even a barking dog. Carver and Peruzzi parked fifty metres down the street and stayed in the car while Brennan and I parked around the corner and went to take a look. We jumped two youths after they came out from the house. One of them was carrying two pouches of heroin. We took them back to Carver and Peruzzi. Carver stayed in the car with them, Peruzzi came with Brennan and me.' Morrissey rubbed the back of his neck.

'Go on,' Rimis said.

'We were going to call in for back-up, but for some crazy reason, Brennan decided to make a fake drug buy so he could get the door open. We watched him walk up the front steps from the bushes by the front fence. Still to this day, I don't know what got into him. Everyone who knew Mickey knew he had a temper on him and took risks. He pushed against the door like a madman and the chain must have snapped because he managed to wedge part of his body in. There was a scuffle. Peruzzi and I ran up to the house, but it was too late by the time we got there; Brennan was lying on the verandah with a bullet to the head.'

'So, what did you do then?'

'We called for an ambulance and back up, like we should have done in the first place. Too late for an ambulance. We dragged his body out onto the street.'

'Did you see Chisca?'

'No, I didn't see him. He could have been there. I heard his name used a couple of times, but mostly they were talking gibberish. I couldn't make out a word they were saying. There was plenty of confusion, screaming and yelling going on. Most of them managed to scamper off out the back door. We nabbed the scum who shot Brennan, but he never told us who else was there that night. I wasn't even sure he was the one who pulled the trigger, even though his prints were all over the gun.'

'Why did Brennan go in alone?'

'I can't give you an answer to that. He was the senior officer. We were waiting for instructions. It all happened so fast. Look, Nick, this is fucking upsetting, dragging all of this up now. It's history. Mickey Brennan's history. Leave it alone. If you want to pin something on Chisca, maybe you can do a deal with him or something, get him to fess up to being there that night.'

'I've already given him a drilling but he's keeping his mouth shut.'

Morrissey stood up. 'Well, that's the end of it then. If Chisca doesn't spill his guts, there's nothing we can do.'

'Yeah, nothing we can do.' Rimis put the file away in his top drawer. He looked at Morrissey and wondered about him. Was the stress of the job getting to him? He seemed preoccupied lately. Rimis knew the combination of the job and personal life was a fine balance. Or was there something else bothering him? Gambling debts? Alcohol problems? A woman on the side causing him grief? 'You going to Otto's Bar tonight? I've got a meeting, so I won't be there till late.'

'No. I'll have to give it a miss. Sophie wants me home, you know what women are like.'

Rimis nodded, but he didn't have the faintest idea what women were like. He had never taken the time to understand them, and until recently, he had never felt the need to.

The first thing Morrissey did when he arrived home was turn on the air con. He was standing in the middle of the kitchen dressed only in a pair of blue and white striped boxer shorts. He snapped the lid off a bottle of a cold beer and took a deep gulp.

It was just after seven and there was no sign of Sophie. She had been working late all week, pulling lots of overtime at the accountant's office where she worked in the city.

He walked over to the fridge and opened it. Left-over roasted chicken, a paper bag of mushrooms, a plastic container of low-fat cream. He didn't usually do the cooking, but tonight he decided he would surprise her. He checked the recipe on the back of a pasta pack then pulled out a saucepan. Spaghetti Carbonara. How hard could it be?

He chopped mushrooms and onions, added a little oil to the frypan. He checked the recipe again, stirred in the cream and went to the fridge and opened another beer.

He leaned back against the bench and watched the sauce simmer. Bloody Rimis. He swallowed, wiped his mouth with the back of his hand. *He* had a hide, lecturing him about his attitude and his drinking. He should talk. How many times had Nick Rimis turned up at the station hung-over from a night on the piss?

Hypocrite.

Chapter Twenty-Four

Jill stood up, pushed the chair away, and walked down a long corridor towards the interview room at North West Metropolitan Region HQ in Parramatta. She wiped the perspiration from her top lip, stepped into the room, shook hands and took a seat across from the three Detective Inspectors. Introductions were made.

'You're aware of the procedure for this interview, Senior Constable?'

Jill looked at the name badge of the less intimidating of the three, committing his name to memory in case she was called upon to use it. She flashed a disarming smile. 'Yes, Sir.'

'Well, let's begin then.'

There were four questions on the sheet in front of her. She placed her hands on her shaking knees to steady them. The first question was so easy she thought she would laugh from the relief. She was being asked to outline the circumstances of aggravation under Section 105A of the Crimes Act.

'Your answer to the first question Senior. When you're ready.'

Jill made a few notes on the paper she had been given.

She sat upright and took a deep breath. She answered in a strong and steady voice. 'The circumstances of aggravation means the alleged offender is armed with an offensive weapon or instrument, the offender is in the company of another person, the alleged uses corporal violence on another person, the alleged offender inflicts bodily harm...' And so she continued, answering every question without hesitation.

Thirty minutes later, Jill walked out of the interview room. She grinned into the mirror in the women's toilet. The interview couldn't have gone better. The panel had nodded and smiled their approval. She punched the air with her fist and smiled at her reflection. She walked out of the building. Rimis had already told her to take the rest of the day off, which suited her; there was someone she had to visit.

She wasn't sure what sort of reception she would receive at Silverwater Correctional Centre, Australia's largest gaol complex. She hated gaols. They were sordid, aggressive places where bad things happened.

'Mr Chisca.' Jill nodded to him before she sat down at the table in front of him in the concrete visits room.

Chisca didn't stand. 'Senior Constable Brennan, or should I call you Jill? I was surprised when I was told I had a visitor today. A friend, I think you said.'

'I don't care what you call me, to be honest; you know this isn't a social visit. I'm here for some answers.' She looked at him and wondered how he felt having to wear the white back-zipped jumpsuit with VISITS in black letters stamped on the back. Whenever she had met him, he had always been impeccably dressed.

'First you must ask the questions.'

Jill squirmed in her seat.

'If you are here about Freddie or that girl, Paloma Browne, let me tell you now, I am an opportunist, I am not a murderer.'

'I'm not here in any official capacity, I'm here to talk to you about my father.' She studied his face for the first time. A thin white scar, which she hadn't noticed before, ran from the corner of his mouth down the length of his chin.

'Yes, your father. You are very much like him. When I first met you, I saw the family resemblance immediately. And you have his temper, I can see.'

'So, you did know him?'

'Yes, I knew Mickey well.' Chisca sat back in his chair and crossed his arms.

'Were you in Lakemba the night he was shot?'

'What sort of question is that?' His face was blank, his eyes cold.

'Try this one then,' Jill frowned. 'Did my father borrow money from you?'

'Are you sure you want to know?' He smiled and Jill could see from the look on his face, he was playing with her. Where was all this going? She looked up at the clock on the wall above Chisca's head and watched the second hand tick by.

'Yes,' she said. 'I want to know.' This was the only chance she would have to find out about her father.

If she didn't, she knew it would haunt her for the rest of her life.

'Sometimes, I believe ignorance is a better alternative.' Chisca leaned forward. She could smell his stale breath. 'After I arrived in Sydney from Melbourne, your father arrested me on a minor charge. We struck a deal. The charge, it was dropped after I provided useful information. We had working relationship which benefitted us both. Not long after, he came to me, asked if I knew anyone who would lend him money. He had gone to banks, but they had all refused him.'

'Did he say why he needed the money?' Jill felt her heart pumping.

'It was to send you to your private school and university.'

Jill stared at him in disbelief. She'd never questioned how her father could afford her expensive education on a detective sergeant's salary.

'Did anyone know about this? I mean, any of his colleagues?'

'I do not know.'

'So where did he get the money from?'

'I gave him names, some associates.' He leant forward and placed his elbows on the table. 'Now it is my turn,' Chisca said.

'What do you mean?'

'I have helped you with your information, now I need you to help me.'

'Well, I don't think there is —'

'That is where you are wrong.'

Jill couldn't believe what was happening here, the

tables had turned. How had she been so naive to think he would give her something for nothing?

'I think I should leave now,' she said. It had been a mistake coming here. Jill stood up and pushed the chair back from the table.

'I want you to tell Detective Morrissey something for me.'

'What do you mean? Why Morrissey?'

'Tell him to watch his back.'

Visiting time was over and when Chisca was led away with the other remand prisoners, he called out to her, 'Tell Morrissey, tell him what I said.'

Jill walked out of the room and slumped against the wall in the corridor. She thought of Morrissey and wondered what part he had really played in her father's death.

It was seven o'clock. Jill walked into Otto's Bar and found Col Morrissey where she expected him to be, sitting up at the bar with a schooner in his hand, watching the day's cricket highlights on the big screen. The place was noisy enough for her to know their conversation wouldn't be overheard.

'Hello Brennan. I'm surprised you wanted to meet here. I didn't think this place was classy enough for you.'

Jill wasn't here for small talk and got right to the point. 'I went to see Dorin Chisca this afternoon.'

Morrissey shifted his gaze from the plasma screen and stared at her. 'You did what?'

'I spoke to Chisca, asked him a few questions about my father.'

Morrissey swore. 'Are you crazy?'

'Maybe I am,' she said. Her mouth curved in a humourless smile. Her heart was racing. She was trying not to show how much Morrissey pissed her off. 'He asked me to give you a message.'

The bar was getting busy; students from the university were gathering at the low tables. 'Well, what's the message?'

'He told me to tell you to watch your back.'

'Fuck,' Morrissey finished the last of his beer in one gulp. 'We're in deep shit here, Brennan.'

Jill pulled up a bar stool beside him and put her bag on the counter. 'What do you mean, *we*?'

'I wasn't there that night in Lakemba. It was a Friday night and I had somewhere else I had to be.'

'None of this makes sense. That's not what you told me the other day. That's not what your statement said.'

'Well, I lied.' Morrissey looked down at his beer. He went to take another mouthful, but realised his glass was empty. 'Chisca told me to meet him at the Lakemba house. Another one, thanks Jimmy,' he called out.

'Why did Chisca want to see you?'

Morrissey looked down at his empty glass. The frown lines on his forehead deepened.

'Come on Sarge, after what I've heard today, whatever you tell me won't come as any surprise to me.'

'I don't want you blabbing what I'm about to tell you to anyone. Do I have your word on that?'

'Depends what it is,' she said.

Morrissey spread his hands out in front of him and tipped over the glass. It rolled towards the edge of the bar but he grabbed it in time before it fell to the floor. 'I was on his payroll and so was Mickey. Chisca was getting nervous, people were threatening him.'

'Was Mickey threatening him? Is that why they shot him?'

'I don't know what went wrong that night, maybe it was an accident. Mickey was hot-headed and had a reputation for taking risks. Maybe, they thought Mickey was me.'

'Why would they think that?'

'Because they were dumb arses, that's why. A month before the stake-out, Blinky came up with this idea to break into Chisca's house in Marrickville and do it over.'

Jimmy placed another beer in front of Morrissey, who took a deep gulp. 'We had a tip-off and knew the house would be empty. Blinky covered for me and I found bundles of money all over the house – in the roof, in cupboards, in panels in the walls. It was the perfect crime. Chisca was never going to report the theft. How could he? And as far as I know, he never suspected me, at least not until now.'

'What happened to the money?'

'Some of it went to Blinky, I took my cut, and the rest of it, Mickey banked into his account.'

'So you're telling me I've been living off ill-gotten gains.'

'Yeah, I guess you have.'

'Does anyone else know about this?' Jill looked at him.

'Scotty knows.'

'Scott Carver? For God's sake, this keeps getting worse.'

'Come on Brennan, you're the lawyer, you've got brains. What are we going to do?'

'Why should I do anything?'

'Because your reputation and Mickey's are at stake.'

'Surprised to see you here Brennan.'

They both turned and looked over their shoulders. It was Rimis. Jill pulled back on her pony-tail.

'How about a drink, Jimmy,' Rimis said.

'Thought you had a meeting? Jill asked.

'Cancelled.'

Jill checked the time on her watch. 'Didn't realise it was so late.' The bar was hot and stuffy and she needed some fresh air. She picked up her shoulder bag and got down from her stool. 'I'll see you two later then. Have a good night.'

Chapter Twenty-Five

Rimis arrived in the office the next morning later than usual. He had spent a quiet evening at home after he left Otto's Bar, drinking a bottle of Hunter Shiraz on his own and watching re-runs of Inspector Morse. He had asked Brennan to come and see him after he had run into her on his way back from the canteen. Five minutes later, she walked into his office carrying a cup of coffee.

'Sit down.' He swung his chair around and clicked onto a file on his computer.

'I've got the DNA results back from those cigarette butts you found at Freddie's gallery.'

'With everything that's happened, I'd forgotten all about them,' she said. 'Did we get a match?'

'The girl must have been a chain smoker, or else she'd been waiting there for a while. Five of the butts belonged to her.'

'And the others?'

'We've eliminated Chisca and Vladu, which is disappointing, but we're still searching the National Data Base.'

'Just because we can't link Chisca and Vladu to the gallery, doesn't mean we can eliminate them completely,' Brennan said.

'You're right.' Rimis stood up from his desk and stretched his arms above his head. 'Chisca is our only lead, but he's not talking. I'm not sure where we go from here.' He looked at Brennan. 'Anything wrong?'

'Nothing I can't handle,' she said.

'Well, if you need to talk to someone, my door's always open.'

'Thanks, boss. Any news on how I went in the Bull Ring?'

'Not yet. I wouldn't worry though, I'm sure you impressed the panel.' He smiled at her. 'How about dinner tonight? I know a good Thai place at Coogee.'

'Thanks, boss, but maybe some other time.'

Rimis turned his attention to the open files on his desk.

'Well, back to it then.'

Brennan slapped her thighs and walked out of his office. 'Yeah, back to it.'

Rimis watched her go, how could he be so stupid? He had just asked a subordinate officer out on a date. He closed his eyes and buried his face in his hands.

Later that evening, Jill walked into her bedroom and dragged out a cardboard archive box from the back of the wardrobe. She sat down on the floor cross-legged, scared of what she might find. This was all that was left of her father, just a box of old papers and photos. She tipped the contents onto the floor, found his warrant of appointment, his driver's licence, even an old library card. And then there were the photos: her mother with a baby in her arms, a few of their wedding, her father in his police uniform taken the day he received the Commissioner's Certificate of Merit.

A road had collapsed during flooding and five members of one family plunged into a creek. They all died, but typical of Mickey Brennan, he tied a rope around his waist and scaled down an embankment to search for any survivors. He had stayed with the bodies until help arrived. She picked up the photo. Tears welled up in her eyes and dripped onto the photo. The day it was taken was the day she had decided she wanted to become a police officer. She had been just ten years old.

At the bottom of the box, in a plastic folder, she found a bundle of bank statements clipped together. She flicked through them until she found one dated April, four years ago, and there it was. Fifty thousand dollars, a cash deposit banked to Mickey's account just as Morrissey had said.

She let the bank statement drop from her hands and tried to think. Had she broken any law? If anybody had, it was Morrissey. And her father? Consorting with a known criminal for starters and who knew what else. No, she didn't believe it, wouldn't believe it. She picked up the photo again. Her father had been a handsome man; she wondered why he never remarried. She recognised her own physical features in his face, the blue eyes and the blonde hair.

She picked up the statements again and looked for a pattern in the withdrawals. The only payments she found were rent payments, credit card payments, and the old Land Cruiser he had on finance. She remembered how much he had loved that car. There were no records of her school fees or university fees. Her father was hopeless with money and record keeping.

If her father had borrowed money from Chisca, it didn't look like it had ever been repaid. She realised he could have paid him in kind, rather than money. He might have done him a favour, turned a blind eye. Chisca wasn't about to tell her anything. She closed her eyes and thought about the fifty-thousand dollars. There was nothing she could do about the money, it was long gone. But what about Morrissey? Who knew what other criminal dealings he was involved in? They both knew if she pointed the finger at him, she would muddy the good name of her father. Morrissey was smarter than he looked. What he had told her about her father undermined everything she thought she had known about him. She pulled herself up from the floor and walked out into the kitchen. She opened the fridge, grabbed a bottle of Pinot Grigio and poured herself a glass. She stood at the kitchen bench and looked out the window at the neighbouring block of apartments. She had never felt so alone. She knew she should go to bed, but she couldn't quite drag herself off yet. She finished her glass of wine, refilled it again and thought back to what Chisca had said about Morrissey watching his back. What had he meant? Was it a threat, or a warning?

Morning came and Jill wondered if she'd be able to get out of bed. If it weren't for sheer will power she would never have made it to the bathroom. She splashed her face with cold water and swept her hair back into a ponytail.

An hour and a half later she was in Chatswood, at her desk. She had taken the time to apply makeup this morning to cover her puffy eyes and hoped nobody would notice how wretched she looked.

She checked her emails, answered the important ones and finished her cup of canteen coffee. She then set about creating two files, one for Paloma Browne, the other for Morrissey. She knew the skills she had learnt when she was practicing law complemented the skills she needed to be a good detective. She had to be persistent, have sound judgement, and be thick-skinned and analytical. Her fingers danced across the keyboard and a few minutes later she sat back and read over her work.

'You're in early, Brennan.' Rimis said.

'Thought I'd try to move some of the backlog.' She put her computer to sleep.

He looked at her. 'You look exhausted.'

'I'm okay.'

'Sure?'

'Really.' She forced a smile and wondered if Rimis knew she was lying.

'Good. Then, I'll leave you to it.'

She turned back to her computer and refreshed the screen. Rimis stopped before he reached his office. 'Brennan? I've had a thought.'

She looked up at him.

'I want you to go to the Union Hotel on the Pacific Highway at North Sydney and ask some questions about Paloma Browne.'

Jill's eyes lit up. 'What do you want me to find out?'

'I want to know more about her. If she was a regular, the staff must have known her, or maybe known the crowd she was mixing with. See what you can find out.'

'But hasn't the Sarge already been there?'

'I want to see if you can come up with any more information.'

Twenty minutes later, Jill walked into the Union Hotel .

'What can I get you?'

'Senior Constable Jill Brennan, Chatswood Police.' Jill flashed her ID at the woman behind the bar.

'The duty manager isn't here. He's gone to the Bank but he should be back soon. The neighbours haven't been complaining about the noise again, have they?'

'I'm not from Licensing. I'm investigating a homicide.'

'Oh?'

'Maybe you can help.' Jill looked at the nametag on the woman's shirt. 'You worked here long, Lynne?'

'About two years now.'

'Can you take a look at this photo and tell me if

you recognise this girl?' Jill pulled a photo out from her bag and placed it on the bar.

'It's Paloma. The poor girl. Everyone here was very upset by what happened.'

'What can you tell me about her?'

'She was a good kid, on the whole. Couple of times we had to refuse her a drink, but she was never any real trouble. Had a small group of friends from the design school down the road. They came in every Friday afternoon, ate at the bistro, stayed late.'

'Was there anyone in particular she mixed with, anyone apart from the design school friends?'

'Only Colin, but I haven't seen him in here since she died.'

'What was this guy Colin like?'

'A charmer, early forties I'd say, too old to be hanging around a young girl like her, but she didn't seem to mind. I think she liked the attention.'

'Gas-bagging again, Lynne?'

'Derek, she's from the police. She's asking about that girl who was murdered, Paloma Browne.'

The manager put his briefcase down on the bar. 'Sorry, but I have to keep an eye on Lynne; she'd stand around yakking all day if I didn't watch her,' he laughed. 'Can you go and tell Ricky I had a call from Sam's Seafood? They can't supply the barramundi this week.'

Lynne disappeared. The manager walked behind the bar and pulled himself a beer. 'Can I get you a drink? On the house, of course.'

'I'm okay thanks.'

'It's muggy outside, don't know how much longer this weather can last. Still it's good for business.'

He lifted the glass to his lips and made a croaking sound when he swallowed. He set his glass down. 'I don't know what else I can tell you about the girl. I've already told your lot everything I know.'

'I appreciate that, but we're still following a line of enquiry. Lynne was telling me about a guy called Colin? Do you know anything about him?'

'Col? Yeah, he's one of your lot.'

'You don't mean Col Morrissey?'

'Yeah, he took my statement. He's been drinking here for years, but stopped coming just before the girl died.'

Jill ran her hand over her mouth. She felt the blood drain from her face.

'You alright love? You look a bit pale. Sure you don't want a drink?'

'No, I'm fine, but I may need to speak to you again.'

'I'm here most days.'

Jill snatched up her bag and almost ran out of the hotel to where she had parked her car. It was time to speak to Rimis and tell him what she knew.

Rimis was at his desk eating a slice of pizza when Jill walked into his office.

'I thought you were on a health kick,' she said.

'I am, but it's all this exercise I've been doing, it's making me hungry.'

Rimis threw what was left of the pizza in the bin and told her to sit down.

'How did you get on at the Union Hotel?'

'I've got some information, but I'm not sure what it means or what I should do with it.'

'You can start by telling me what you've got.'

She closed the door and sat down.

'Well then, what's this all about?'

Brennan bit her lip. 'The Sarge knew Paloma Browne.'

'Morrissey?'

She sat back in her chair and wondered what Rimis would make of what she'd just said. 'He was a regular at the Union. I don't know what their relationship was exactly, but he bought her dinner and drinks every Friday night, right up until a few weeks before she disappeared.'

Rimis filled his cheeks with air and released his breath slowly. He stood up from his desk and paced the room, stopped and looked at her. 'Tell Morrissey I want to see him. Now!'

Morrissey walked into Rimis's office ten minutes later. 'Brennan said you wanted to see me.'

'Sit down.' Rimis said.

'Something wrong? What have I done now?'

'I said, sit down.'

'Look, if it's about what happened with Choi in the canteen yesterday, I —'

'It's Paloma Browne,' Rimis said.

'Oh yeah? What have we found out?'

'Why didn't you tell me you were involved with her?'

Morrissey got to his feet. 'How did you find out?'

'Don't worry about that. You're in deep shit, you know that, don't you? You're a bloody idiot. Why didn't you tell me upfront you were involved with the girl?'

'I was worried about how it would look, and if Sophie ever found out —'

'Were you having sex with her?' Rimis asked.

'No, of course not. I just met the girl at the pub on Friday nights. We had a few drinks, a few laughs, that's all.'

'You better not be lying to me.'

'Christ Nick, she was only twenty. I'm old enough to be her father.'

'Get out of my sight. I have to work out what I'm going to do about this.'

Morrissey turned to leave. 'Come on, Nick. Don't tell me if some young pretty thing paid you attention you wouldn't be in for it.'

'Get out,' Rimis yelled. A moment later there was a knock on the door. 'What is it?' Rimis bellowed.

Brennan opened the door. 'Can I talk to you, boss?' Brennan asked.

'Come in.' He picked up a file and slapped it down again on the desk.

'I need to talk to you, but not here at the Station.'

Rimis took a deep breath and brought himself back into line. He saw the concerned look on her face. 'My offer's still open for dinner.'

Jill nodded.

He scribbled the address on a yellow post-it note and handed it to her. 'Is seven o'clock okay?' he asked.

'See you then.' Jill looked at the note and closed the door behind her on her way out.

Rimis stared at the back of the door and wondered if what she wanted to talk to him about had anything to do with Morrissey.

There was ample parking on Coogee Bay Road. Jill had allowed herself plenty of time because she didn't know what the traffic would be like. She had twenty minutes to spare before she was due to meet Rimis so she decided to go for a walk to Dolphin Point to clear her head.

Coogee Beach, although beautiful, was a dangerous place to swim, especially when there were huge seas. The beach dropped off suddenly at the water's edge with a dangerous shore break. She had read somewhere that Coogee Beach caused more spinal injuries than any other beach in Australia.

When she came here as a child with her father, they always swam at the northern end of the beach, in the old Giles Baths which was now an open rock pool. There were still people swimming. A group of boys were playing beach cricket. A few girls in skimpy bikinis lay flat out on towels. Barking dogs off their leads were following couples walking hand in hand along the water's edge.

She walked up to the headland and stood in front

of the Bali memorial. Eighty-eight Australians had died in the 2002 Bali bombing. Twenty of them had lived in Coogee and the neighbouring suburbs.

Jill stood still and looked out at the ocean. How easily lives could be altered, changed forever by a single act. She thought about her father and about the people who had lost their lives in Bali.

She knew she had to tell Rimis about Morrissey and her father, about their involvement with Chisca. Her career was all Jill had. She knew Morrissey well enough to know he would try to implicate her in some way. How would she explain away the fifty- thousand dollars? She decided to ring Thomas, Munroe and West in the morning and make an appointment to see the senior partner, Max West. Perhaps he would have some answers for her.

Rimis was sitting in a quiet corner at the back of the room when she walked into the Thai restaurant. She was on time, he was early. He stood up when he saw her and she was surprised when he pulled her chair out for her.

She sat down. 'I've been down at the beach. It's beautiful this time of day, especially up at the Point.' Jill picked up the menu and studied it.

'See anything you like?' Rimis asked.

She put the menu down on the table. Jill watched him study the menu. 'You order,' she said. He looked at her and she quickly looked away. She reminded herself Rimis was her boss. This really wasn't a date, she silently told herself. She had to remain professional, detached.

After Rimis ordered for them and a bottle of decent Claret arrived, he looked across the table at her.

'So what's so important you couldn't tell me at the Station?'

Jill took a small sip of her wine, leaned back against her chair.

'It's the Sarge. I think he murdered Paloma.' She watched for his reaction.

Rimis raised his eyebrows. 'You don't pull any punches do you?'

'Don't look at me like that. I'm serious.'

'Alright, then. Tell me why you think Senior Sergeant Colin Morrissey is a murderer?'

'You're making fun of me.'

'I'm sorry,' he said. 'Give me your thoughts.'

'If you look at this case from a different angle, it all makes sense.' Jill leaned into the table. 'I've been thinking it through. You know the note I found in Freddie's office?'

Rimis nodded.

'We assumed the *both* meant Freddie and Calida, but what if Paloma was trying to blackmail Morrissey and Chisca? If the relationship Paloma had with Morrissey was more than friendship, he might have told her Chisca was up to more than just selling a few paintings. Calida worked it out, so why wouldn't a bright girl like Paloma Browne work it out as well?'

'But how did the note end up in Freddie's office?'

'Paloma used to work at the Gallery, remember? She might have left the note there. Freddie found it, misunderstood it and disregarded it. Or maybe

Paloma thought Freddie was in on it, but changed her mind later.'

'It's a bit far-fetched. I know he's guilty of a lot of things, but Col Morrissey? Murder?'

'If the stakes were high enough, I think he would do just about anything,' she said.

'But he was having a relationship with the girl. I don't know. I can't see him doing it, I don't think he has the stomach for it.'

'Okay, then. What if Vladu murdered her and Morrissey was just the delivery man.'

'You're clutching at straws now.' Rimis raised his eyebrows.

She was about to tell him of the hold Morrissey had over her, when two steaming bowls of noodles arrived. They picked up their chopsticks and ate in silence. She pushed aside her bowl. 'There's something else I have to tell you.'

'What? There's more.'

Jill avoided his eyes when she told him what Morrissey had told her about her father's involvement with Chisca and the fifty-thousand dollars deposited into his account.

Silence.

'Aren't you going to say something?' She looked into his eyes, searching for a reaction.

'I'm thinking,' Rimis said. He drummed his chopsticks on the side of his bowl. 'Paloma was meeting someone at the gallery. The cigarette butts place her there. If only we could get a match on the other butts.' He put the chopsticks down on the table and looked at her. 'You know I have to report Morrissey. I can't let him get away with this, but first, I'll ask him if he's got an alibi for the night Paloma was murdered. And I wouldn't worry about the money. It's been four years, and from what you've told me, Chisca is unlikely to make a noise about it. Make a donation to your favourite charity if your conscience is bothering you. Maybe we can talk to Morrissey, ask him to keep quiet about it. It's not only you; Bill Peruzzi's widow is affected by this business too.'

The waiter came over to ask if they wanted coffee or dessert, or something else to drink.

Rimis looked at Jill.

She shook her head. 'No, I've had enough,' she said. She looked around. The place was empty, apart from the two of them and the staff. She slung her bag over her shoulder. 'Morrissey's got something to do with Paloma's death, I'm sure of it,' she said. She swirled what was left of her wine in the glass then put it down. Rimis finished his off.

'Don't go jumping to conclusions just because you want this case solved,' Rimis said.

Brennan paid her half of the bill in cash and Rimis paid the remainder on his credit card. With his hand on the small of her back he guided her out into the airless night. Despite the heat, she shivered at his touch. She fumbled inside her bag for her keys.

There was a beat of awkward silence and for a moment Jill thought he was going to kiss her.

'See you tomorrow,' he said.

As she drove off, she looked in the rear view mirror. Nick Rimis had his phone to his ear and was staring after her.

Chapter Twenty-Six

Rimis walked into Otto's Bar. It was lunch time. The place was deserted. 'Thought I'd find you here.' Rimis sat down on his usual bar stool beside Morrissey and ran his hands along the polished surface.

'You got a problem with me having a quiet beer?'

'Thought you were supposed to be getting yourself sorted,' Rimis said.

'Yeah, well.' Morrissey shifted on his stool.

'I've been talking to Brennan,' Rimis said.

'And what does Miss Super Cop, have to say?' Morrissey gave Rimis a mock salute.

'Let me order a drink first. Jimmy, give me a soda water.' He looked at Morrissey. 'I'd ask if you wanted another one, but by the look of you, I think you've already had one too many.'

'Maybe I have. What's it to you?' Morrissey made a snorting noise.

'Just make sure you sober up before you get into your car and drive back to work.'

'What do you want? Someone else complain about me?' Morrissey asked. He tipped his glass up and emptied it. Morrissey's mouth turned downwards. He pushed a bowl of peanuts around the bar. He looked at Rimis. 'Just say what you have to say and leave me alone.'

'I wanted to ask you about Brennan and her father. She told me about this business between him and Chisca.'

Morrissey looked at Rimis. 'I misjudged her. I thought she'd keep her mouth shut.' Morrissey grabbed a fist-full of peanuts and jammed them in his mouth. 'So, you going to report me?'

'I should.' Rimis said.

'I know you should, but are you going to?'

Rimis's phone vibrated in his pocket. He had turned it to silent so he wouldn't be interrupted. He pulled it out and checked the caller ID. 'I want you to tell me you've got an alibi for the night Paloma Browne was murdered.'

'What the fuck is this?' Morrissey covered his face with his hands.

Rimis looked at Morrissey. 'Just answer the question. Where were you that night between eight-thirty and midnight?'

Morrissey let his hands drop. 'At home.'

'With Sophie?'

'Her sister was sick. She was staying at her place to help look after the kids. I didn't know I needed an alibi. And don't look at me like that. You don't seriously think I killed her do you?'

'Well somebody did. I want to find out who.'

'Go fuck yourself.'

Rimis didn't bother with his soda water when it arrived. He stood up. He'd had enough of Morrissey.

He threw a five dollar note on the bar. He would speak to him again when he was sober. He walked outside, passed Morrissey's parked car and remembered Brennan saying something about seeing a car the night Paloma was murdered. He dialled her mobile.

'Brennan?'

'Yes, boss?'

'You said a car was parked in Jones Street, in front of yours, the night Paloma was murdered.'

'That's right.'

'You never said what the make or colour was.'

'It was dark but I'm pretty sure it was a Ford Fiesta. Red, I think.'

Rimis ended the call and looked down at Morrissey's 2010 red Ford Fiesta and slapped his hand on the roof of the car. Rimis's phone vibrated again and this time he answered it. 'Peter?'

'Hi Nick, how are things?' Rimis heard no emotion in his brother's voice. He knew he didn't really care what was happening in his life. Besides, Peter Rimis knew the answer to the question before he'd even asked it: work, work and more work.

'Busy right now,' Rimis replied.

'Listen Nick, it's Mum. I thought you should know, she's not well. Maybe you could pop in and see her. It would mean a lot to her.'

'I'll see what I can do, but things are pretty hectic. We're in the middle of investigating a double homicide.'

'Yeah, well sometimes the living are owed more attention than the dead, Nicko. Might pay to remember that.'

Rawlings walked up to Rimis in the corridor. He looked flustered and was carrying a file in his arms. 'Boss, I don't suppose you've seen the Sarge anywhere have you? I've called his mobile, but it just goes to voicemail. We're supposed to be following up a lead on Taggart. A barmaid at the Cauliflower Hotel reckons she remembers seeing him talking to a guy who fits Vladu's description.'

'What?' Rimis looked at him.

'The Sarge, have you seen him?'

'Yeah, I've seen him. Better take Choi with you to talk to the barmaid.'

Rimis walked into his office and dialled Morrissey's number. 'Come on Col, pick up the bloody phone.' He frowned and called Otto's Bar next and spoke to Jimmy. Jimmy told him Morrissey had left the bar five minutes after he had. He was drunk and Jimmy had called him a taxi. He said he was going home to sleep it off. Rimis threw his phone on his desk, put his hands on his hips and paced the room.

Brennan rushed into his office.

'What is it now? He frowned.

'You know those cigarette butts I found outside Freddie's gallery? I ran them through the AFP Data Base. We've got a match.'

'Well? Who do they belong to?'

'Morrissey.'

A police truck pulled up behind Rimis and Brennan

outside Morrissey's house in Dundas. Rimis and Brennan got out of their car. Brennan cleared her throat. 'You got a plan?'

'Nope,' Rimis replied. The heat had plastered his hair to his head. He looked towards the house and pulled his phone from his pocket. He dialled Morrissey's home number. It answered on the fourth ring.

Silence.

'Col, it's me, Nick. I'm here, outside your house.' Rimis saw Morrissey's silhouette through a gap in the lacy curtains. He had his phone to his ear.

'How did you know I'd be here?'

'Jimmy told me. Is Sophie in there with you?' Rimis ran his tongue over his lips.

'She's still at work.'

'You want to come out and talk about this?'

'There's nothing to talk about. We both know what happens next.'

'Col, we need to talk about your situation.'

'Don't practice your negotiator skills on me, Nick. I've had more practice than you.' The call ended.

Rimis threw his hands in the air and paced the footpath. When he had calmed down, he considered his options. He could go up to the front door and deal with the situation calmly, but from the way Morrissey sounded on the phone, that was out of the question. Rimis looked at Brennan. 'He'll have his service revolver with him. Ring for backup. Tell them to turn off their sirens.' Rimis looked up the street. The blue flashing lights had already drawn the crowds.

Less than ten minutes later, Sophie Morrissey tried to drive into the street but was stopped by a burly police officer. She wound down her window and demanded to know what was happening.

'I'm his wife,' she told him. 'You have to let me through.'

'Can I see your driver's license please, madam?' He handed her licence back to her. 'I'm sorry, Mrs Morrissey. You can park your car here and Constable Reilly will take you to Inspector Rimis.'

Rimis saw Sophie approaching.

'Nick, what the hell's happening here? I got a call from one of the neighbours about Col, that he's —'

'It's alright, Sophie, we'll sort it.'

'I want to talk to him.'

'I'm not sure that's a good idea,' Rimis said.

'What do you mean? I'm his wife, for Christ sake. If he's going to listen to anybody, it'll be me.' A look of obstinacy flashed across her face.

Rimis sighed. He knew there was no use arguing with Sophie Morrissey. 'Okay then, but keep him calm. See if you can get him to talk to me.'

Sophie dragged her mobile phone from her handbag and turned her back on Rimis. With her head low, she spoke into the phone. The conversation only lasted a few minutes. Sophie ended the call and returned to where Rimis was standing.

'He'll speak to you. Nobody else.'

Rimis walked up the front steps of the house and knocked firmly. He knew the house; he'd been to dinner here a few times. The door opened. Morrissey looked out and stepped aside. The television was on in the lounge room. The volume was turned down.

'Come into the kitchen,' Morrissey said.

The two men sat down opposite each other at the kitchen table. Morrissey's service revolver lay next to a tattered newspaper, open at the sports pages, while a half-empty bottle of Bourbon nudged a white saucer filled with stubbed cigarette butts.

'Want a drink?' Morrissey's voice slurred.

'No,' Rimis said. 'Too early in the day for me.'

Morrissey removed the last of the cigarettes from the open pack and put it between his teeth. He lit up and blew smoke towards the ceiling.

'Come on, Col. Tell me what this is all about. It's all going to come out now anyway.'

Morrissey didn't move. He just stared at the empty glass in front of him.

Rimis spoke to him in a quiet voice.

'For Christ's sake, Col. I know most of it anyway, just fill in the gaps. Make it easy on yourself; at least have a thought for Sophie. She's out there in front of all the neighbours, worried half to death.'

Morrissey dropped his voice to a whisper. 'If she hadn't turned up, none of it would have happened.'

'What do you mean? If who hadn't turned up?'

'Paloma.' Morrissey ran his hand through his greasy, unwashed hair. 'Chisca and I were in his warehouse office and we didn't see her arrive. She'd come by to drop off some of her Whiteleys. When she walked into the storeroom she found traces of cocaine on the floor. She had a real nose for it, knew the quality stuff.

I had trouble explaining what I was doing there. She was a smart girl and it didn't take her long to put two and two together.' Morrissey poured himself another drink.

'So what happened then?'

'Like I said, she was smart. It must have been then that the idea of blackmail came to her. Chisca told me she thought Freddie was in on it as well, but Freddie had no idea what was going on.'

'What happened the night she was murdered?'

'I didn't kill her. You've got to believe me. She was supposed to be meeting Chisca in the car park at Freddie's gallery for the payoff, but Chisca sent me instead. When I told her I didn't have the money, she went ballistic. I tried to reason with her, warn her off, but she wouldn't listen. Then Vladu turned up. That's when I walked away, turned my back on her and left her with him. I don't know what happened then. Maybe she put up a fight and it all got out of hand. Who knows? Vladu could have been under instructions to make her disappear, to make the problem go away.' Morrissey buried his face in his hands. 'You have to believe me. I thought Vladu would probably rough her up a bit. I didn't think he would kill her.'

Rimis sat back. 'Christ Col, this is serious stuff.'

Morrissey slumped forward onto the table and buried his head in his arms. 'I'm fucked.'

'Yeah, mate, you certainly are.'

Twenty minutes later, the streetlights came on. The flashing lights of the police vehicles and the ambulances were all the more spectacular because of the fading light. Brennan was holding Sophie Morrissey's arm when Col Morrissey walked down the front steps with Rimis by his side. His cuffed wrists were out in front of him and when he walked past Sophie, all he could say to her was, 'Sorry, Soph.'

Chapter Twenty-Seven

Jill showered, put on a tracksuit and made herself a strong coffee. She was looking forward to a quiet evening at home. When she first started working with Rimis he had told her she would have to learn detachment or else she would burn out. Great advice coming from him, she thought. She had noticed a change in him recently, the way he behaved around her was different from the way he had been when she first met him. She wondered what his interests were and if they had anything in common apart from the job. One thing she did know about him, he was like a dog with a bone when it came to a case.

The lamps came on automatically in the lounge-room. It was almost seven-thirty. She picked up her car keys and shoulder bag from the table beside the front door and left.

She hadn't felt like cooking tonight and had decided on pizza instead. She couldn't believe her luck when she found a parking space on Campbell Parade right outside Papa Giovanni's. She ordered a small marinara pizza with extra cheese and crossed the road to the park opposite, content to wait the twenty minutes until her order was ready.

She sat down on a slatted timber bench and kicked off her shoes. A group of seagulls were fighting over a split bag of chips in front of her. She shooed them away.

The wind whipped back her hair; her eyes watered and the seagulls squalled overhead. She stretched her bare feet out in front of her and watched the passers-by enjoying the remnants of what had been a perfect day. Dog-walkers, joggers, people of all ages, young and old, all levels of fitness passed in front of her. A small white dog ran over to her, panting. It sniffed at the chips, wagged its tail. She reached down and scratched his head. He licked her hand and bounded off.

Jill couldn't imagine living anywhere else. She had surfed here with her father. Most weekends they would just hang out, eat greasy fish and chips from waxy, white paper wrappings. Images came back to her: waves pounding against the shore, her father hauling her up onto his strong shoulders, lumps of sand in her swimming costume at the end of the day. She blinked back the tears. Whoever said time heals all wounds didn't know what they were talking about. Memories, even the good ones, hurt.

She walked up the stairs to her apartment and the smell of pizza trailed behind her. She unlocked the front door, walked into the kitchen and opened the fridge. An opened bottle of her favourite Pinot Grigio was lying on its side on the middle shelf. It was a good drop for the money; dry and cool. She unscrewed the lid and poured. Against the window sill was an empty line of wine bottles. She had meant to take them down to the recycling bin before she had gone out for pizza.

A voice inside her head told her she was drinking too much. The National Health Guidelines recommended one standard drink a day for women and two alcohol free days a week. She opened the kitchen windows. She was hoping for a sea breeze to cool the apartment. A party was in full swing on the floor below; muffled voices, thumping music. There was a loud knock at the front door.

She threw the last piece of pizza crust into the box and reached for the bottle to refill her glass. She checked the time on her watch. It was close to eight-thirty. She hoped it wasn't her neighbours downstairs, come to invite her to their party. She put her wine glass down and walked out of the kitchen to the front door.

The building didn't have a security intercom system. She had spoken to the strata managers about it when she'd first moved in, but they had told her there wasn't enough money in the building fund to cover it. She pulled back the security chain and wondered if it was William. She realised she hadn't phoned him to thank him for the flowers.

Kevin Taggart was standing in the doorway with his hands in his pockets. He was wearing a heavy coat. She looked into his watery eyes.

'Are you going to invite me in? I need to speak to you,' he said.

Jill wondered if she should call Rimis but knew

this was her chance to speak to Kevin alone. If anyone could find out what was going on his life, it was her. She closed the door. The brass security chain rattled when she opened it again. She looked at the scratches on his face. 'What happened to you?'

Kevin ignored her. 'I need to talk.' He wiped the sweat from his forehead and pushed past her.

Jill sat down on the ottoman and fidgeted with her hair. 'You okay?'

Kevin sat down opposite her in the middle of the sofa. His knees were twitching; he looked pale and drawn as if he hadn't slept for days. Then the expression on his face changed. A faint smile appeared on his lips. He sat back on the sofa, as if he expected to stay there for some time. 'Your boss, Nick Rimis, he's a good copper that one. Sharp as a tack. From the first time we met, I knew he'd made up his mind about me.'

Jill shifted on the ottoman and placed her hands on her knees. 'Inspector Rimis would like to speak to you. I, we…'

He was staring past her with glazed eyes and Jill realised she was looking at madness, plain and simple.

'Kevin?' Jill frowned. 'Did you hear what I just said?'

When he spoke to her, he lowered his voice; it was almost a whisper. 'After Edi and Rhoda, I thought it was the end of it. I went back to living my life and I didn't think about them again. With the money they left me, I was going to disappear. I wanted to start a new life, escape the past, leave the bad memories behind.'

Jill's heart was in her throat.

'No one was more shocked than me when I won the Wynne. People, important people, noticed me for the first time in my life. I had a chance to do something decent for once. Then I met Freddie Winfred.' He reached into his pocket and pulled out a small, empty syringe, held it between his thumb and index finger and tapped it lightly against his leg. His hands were shaking. He looked around him, over his shoulder, towards the front door. The music and noise from downstairs were getting louder. The party was in full swing.

Jill had thought Rimis had it all wrong about Kevin, but he was right. She looked at the scratch marks on his face and knew she had to stay calm.

There was a knock at the door.

'See who it is and get rid of them.'

Kevin followed her to the door and whispered, 'I'll be standing right behind you with this.' Kevin traced the point of the syringe against her neck and edged closer to her.

Jill opened the door as wide as the brass chain would allow. 'William. What are you doing here?'

'I've been thinking about what happened the other night and —'

Jill heard the conciliatory tone in his voice. 'It's not me you should be saying sorry to,' she said. 'Go and phone him. I don't want to talk to you, it's Sunday! Do you hear me? It's Sunday!' Jill slammed the door in his face and waited for the sound of him leaving. She stepped back. Kevin flipped the catch, locking them in. The madness was gone, at least for the moment. Perhaps she had imagined the whole thing and he was playing some sick, cruel joke on her. He told her to come away from the door and they walked back into the middle of the room.

'Boyfriend trouble?'

'Why are you here, Kevin? Why are you doing this?'

Kevin wasn't listening. He scratched his arms through his coat. He was pacing backwards and forwards. He turned to her. 'I want to explain everything to you before I leave,' he said. There was a silent pause. 'My mother was a very troubled woman. Can you believe a son could hate his mother enough to kill her?'

'Some sons could,' Jill said.

Kevin slumped down onto the lounge, threw his head back and stared at Jill. 'I was in the back seat when a truck ran a red light. It crashed into the driver's side of the family's station wagon. It was my fifth birthday. Ever heard that song, *Right or Left at Oak Street?*

'No.' Jill edged herself onto the ottoman. If she could only keep him talking there may be a way out of this.

'It's about making choices. Turn right, turn left?' He hummed a few bars of the song.

'Your mother blamed you for your father's death, didn't she?'

He stopped humming and looked at her as if she was mad. 'I blamed myself. He took the long way home; he was going to take me to the park so I could play on the equipment. I remember I had been pestering him all day. If he hadn't, we wouldn't have been at that intersection. That's why I never stood up to my mother. I took whatever she dished out, all the punishments, all the abuse. All those wasted years.' Kevin shook his head. 'But then, I couldn't take it anymore.'

Kevin pulled out a worn, brown leather diary from the inside of his coat pocket and threw it on the coffee table in front of her. 'Take a look if you want, they're all there; she wrote all the punishments down in that book. I keep it to remind myself of how evil she was. My mother was filled with feelings that ate away at her. In the end they destroyed her, just like they destroyed me.'

She flicked through the diary and when she handed the diary back to him, she watched his paw-like hands caress the cover, as if it was in some way holy. His breathing was more even now and he closed his eyes. When he didn't speak, Jill wondered if he had fallen asleep. She shifted on the ottoman and tried to stand.

His eyes flicked open and he leant forward and returned the diary to his coat pocket. 'Don't you want to know how I did it? How I killed her?'

'You're going to tell me anyway.'

'Chest pains. She got me to take her to see her doctor. When I was in the waiting room, I picked up a medical journal on venous embolisms. Never heard of them before then. These embolism things got me thinking. I read up on how to find an artery.

'It was a Sunday, I put the kettle on as usual and after she dozed off on the sofa, I took an empty hypodermic syringe, ran my fingers slowly down her neck until I felt her pulse and injected it into the artery.

The carotid artery, you heard of it? It only took a few minutes. She never said a word.'

'What about Edi and Rhoda Blake?'

Kevin frowned. 'Those two were too proud for their own good. And they were like me, nobody cared whether they lived or died. I did them a favour. Edi was losing her marbles anyway, and Rhoda wasn't far behind.'

'But didn't you feel anything, after you'd killed them?'

Kevin spoke in a small voice. 'I returned to my life without another thought. Locked the memories away in a little black box in my head.'

Jill had to lean forward to hear his words. She knew that if she got out of this alive, she would never doubt Nick Rimis's instincts again. She drew in a deep breath. 'Tell me about Freddie.'

'Freddie?' His mood changed and he laughed. 'I liked her at first, then I found out what sort of woman she really was.'

'What do you mean?'

'You've met her. She was always showing herself off, flaunting herself. Mutton dressed up as lamb.'

Jill looked puzzled. 'The way she dressed was no reason to kill her.'

'She rang me, wanted me to come and pick her up from her gallery. The battery in her van had died and she wanted to drop off a painting at Chisca's warehouse. She told me she wanted to take one last look at *North Coast Summers* before it left the country. I knew Chisca was going back to Romania for good and was taking my watercolour with him. She was flustered when I picked her up and couldn't stop talking about the painting, or Chisca. I got the feeling she was infatuated with him. We got to the warehouse and she became agitated when she realised she'd left her phone at the gallery.

'We went inside. Freddie unlocked the storeroom and unwrapped the painting she'd brought with her. I was shocked when I saw it. It was an innuendo of *North Coast Summers*. At first, I didn't know whether to be flattered or angry, so I told her it was a good copy and we both had a laugh.'

'So why did she take you to the warehouse?'

Kevin squirmed in his seat. 'She wanted to swap the original. At first, I thought she was joking, and then I saw the greed in her eyes and knew she was serious. I thought she appreciated my talent, liked me for who I was, but it was the money she was after. Freddie was all fired up and tried to convince me Chisca wouldn't notice, but I wasn't so sure. He'd told me the painting reminded him of a place in Romania where he'd spent family holidays when he was a boy. I even looked it up on *Google Earth,* but I think he saw something in it that I didn't, because it looked nothing like the place.'

'What was Freddie going to do with the original?'

'She was going to sell it and share the spoils with me. She wanted me to take over from where Chisca left off and use my reputation to push her sister's innuendos. I tried to talk her out of it. She asked me what the harm in it was, if he was leaving the country. She said Chisca would be long gone before he noticed the difference. Her plan was to sell them on the overseas market, but I told her I wasn't interested.

A lot of time and effort had gone into painting *North Coast Summers*. Then she laughed at me, told me I was a fool because I could make good money. Said she had made a killing with Chisca and she didn't want it to stop. She started talking about money laundering. I didn't get what she was on about and told her I wouldn't be part of it. Then she laughed at me again. It was that laugh of hers that did it. When I first heard it at the Archibald, it reminded me of the way my mother laughed at me, and when I heard it again at the warehouse, something came over me. I snapped. I was surprised, she put up a good fight.' Kevin ran his fingers over the welts on his cheek.

'Did her sister know what she was up to with Chisca?'

'Who? Calida? No,' he laughed. 'Freddie told me she didn't have any idea what was going on.'

'So what happened to the original?'

'After I killed Freddie, I thought about what she had said. I took it and left the copy. I was surprised when I picked up the painting, I didn't remember it being so heavy. I pulled part of the frame away. It all made sense then. It was the drugs Chisca's clients were after, not the art. I don't know what happened to the paintings once the drugs were removed from the frames; I suppose they were sold on eBay or used for land fill.'

'Did Freddie know what Chisca was up to?'

'I don't think it would have entered her stupid little head. Chisca was paying her good money for the innuendos.'

'Kevin, let's talk to Nick Rimis. I'm sure —'

'I'm tired of talking.' He moved closer to her and ran his open hand down her face. His expression changed. He looked as if he'd woken up in the middle of a nightmare. Perspiration was streaming down the side of his face.

Jill had bought herself some time, but she knew she had to keep him talking at least until she worked out what she was going to do next. Before the undercover assignment took her away from general duties police work, she'd come up against men like Kevin Taggart; men who were out of control, either from drugs, alcohol or mental illness. There was no way to stop them because they had nothing left to lose. Kevin was menacing her with the syringe, trying to unnerve her.

'Kevin you don't need to do this. I thought we were friends,' Jill said as a knot of fear pushed up from her throat.

'Friends? Some friend. You're boring me now.'

'It was Freddie we were after, Kevin. I went undercover to —'

'I don't want to hear it. I don't want to hear any of it.'

Jill tried to imagine what Rimis would do if he was here in this room with them now.'

Kevin started to sing the song, 'Turn left…'

Jill was thinking hard now, trying to come up with ways to distract him. Isn't that what Rimis had taught her? Her service revolver was in the bedroom.

Kevin stepped closer. 'Don't get any ideas.' The staleness of his breath was overpowering.

She considered her options. Kevin was solidly built with heavy shoulders, but he wasn't particularly fit.

She wasn't sure what his reflexes were like, but after three glasses of wine, she knew she couldn't rely on hers. Whatever she decided to do, she had to act quickly. She wondered what he was waiting for. Why didn't he just jab her and be done with it?

'You know why I have to kill you?' Kevin spat flecks of saliva at her.

Jill shook her head.

Kevin wiped his hands on his shirt and ran his tongue over his lips. 'You lied to me about leaving the police; you told me you liked my paintings, but you were only using me to get to Freddie. I trusted you, liked you, but you're just like all the rest.' He rushed towards her.

Jill dropped to the floor, rolled onto her side and stood up again in time to deliver a swift kick. He buckled over. The look on his face told her that, like most men, he had underestimated her. *Service revolver.* She ran towards the bedroom.

Eyes wide with pain, he followed after her, grabbed her from behind and delivered a swift punch to the side of her head. She staggered, moaned and stumbled forwards. He grabbed her hair and slammed her face into the floorboards. Crack. Bloodied nose, stinging eyes, legs folded beneath her. A kick to her ribs.

Kevin gritted his teeth. Another kick to her ribs. He straddled her, pinned her down with his full weight. Bright lights, taste of blood, thumping in her head. *Get the fuck off me,* Jill opened her mouth to scream. *Get the fuck off me!* But the words didn't come.

Chapter Twenty-Eight

The unrenovated, Californian bungalow where Rimis lived was in a quiet, leafy street, three blocks back from Maroubra Beach. His mobile phone rang. He sat upright on the floral, high winged chair, which had once belonged to his mother. The lights were all on, the TV was blaring. He picked up the remote control and pressed *mute*.

Yawn.

'Hello,' he said. He checked the time on the DVD player. Nine-fifteen.

'Nick? It's William Phillips.'

Rimis heard the panic in William's voice. He stood up from his chair, ran his hand through his hair.

'It's Jill. I'm outside her apartment. I went to see her tonight, but before I had a chance to say anything to her, she told me to phone someone. She didn't say who, but I took a guess and rang you. She wasn't making any sense. There was something about the way she spoke to me. I could tell she was scared, really scared.'

Rimis swallowed. 'She alright?'

'Don't know. Maybe it's worth you coming over.'

'Did she say anything to you?'

'Yeah, she was going on about it being Sunday,

made a big fuss about it. But what that's got to do with anything?'

'Stay where you are.'

Ten minutes later Rimis's Commodore screeched to a stop behind William's parked car. He jumped out. 'Wait here,' he yelled.

'I'm coming with you.'

'I need you to stay here for when back up arrives, tell them where I am.'

Rimis knew as well as any officer did, the procedure was to wait for back up, but Jill's life was at stake here. He sprinted up the stairs two at a time and thumped against the door with his fist.

No answer.

Seconds later, he took a step back before leaning into his kick and driving his heel into the door. He looked across the room. Jill was out cold on the floor, her legs splayed flat against the floor; Kevin was saddling her, holding a syringe in his hand.

Rimis looked from Jill's inert body to Kevin and every instinct told him to react, but he knew he had to stay calm.

'Put it down Kevin, nice and slow now.'

'I'll do it. I'll kill her, one jab in the right spot will do it.'

'You don't want to do this. It's over, it's finished with. People will understand.'

'Understand? I'm beyond having anyone understand me, you and I both know that.' Kevin's voice choked.

'Put the syringe down, we'll talk.'

Sirens in the street.

Kevin's eyes narrowed. 'Got to you, didn't it?'

'What do you mean?'

'What I did to Edi and Rhoda.'

'They didn't deserve to die.' Rimis kept his anger in check.

'I knew if their deaths looked accidental, I'd get away with it. But Freddie, I made a mistake with her.'

William rushed up behind Rimis. 'What the hell's going on?'

Rimis held one arm up to block him from advancing any further. He could hear the shuffle of feet on the stairs, neighbouring doors being opened, closed again. The music that was so loud when he'd first arrived, now suddenly quiet. He looked at William from the corner of his eye. 'Thought I told you to stay put,' he said.

Rimis took in the room, the upturned coffee table, the curtains pulled from their tracks and the standing lamp lying on the floor next to him. He was proud of her; she had given Taggart a run for his money.

Brennan stirred, groaned. She turned her head to one side and Rimis locked onto her eyes to give her some reassurance. Brennan had seemed so tough when she'd first started this assignment, but recently, he'd seen another side to her.

Kevin looked at Rimis and shook his head. 'My mother. You've got no idea what it was like being controlled by her. But I'm the one who's in control now.'

'It was a long time ago, Kevin.' Rimis took a step towards him.

'Stay where you are, or I'll use this.' Kevin stabbed the air with the syringe.

'What would your father think if he could see

you now? What would he say if he knew what you'd turned into?'

Kevin's eyes widened, he rolled his head to one side and bellowed like a wounded animal. 'Shut up. Don't talk about him. Shut up, shut up,' he shouted. Horrible sobs erupted; an outpouring of pain, self-loathing, torment.

'Get off her Kevin. I'm not telling you again. Get off her *now!*'

Kevin raised his arm in the air, ready to strike. Without pause, Rimis squeezed out a single shot. It hit Kevin in the side of his neck.

Kevin rolled off Jill and landed on his back on the floor beside her. A slow wet stain appeared on his trousers. Urine. His body was stretched out on the floor, like a Salvador Dali painting. It had happened too fast. Rimis's nostrils filled with the smell of cordite. He walked over and crouched down beside Kevin. His face was a mess. He felt for a pulse before removing the syringe from Kevin's fist.

Brennan opened her eyes but closed them again. He heard her shallow breathing. He cradled her head. 'Jill, for God's sake, say something.' He called her name again and brushed her hair back from her face.

'Nick?'

'It's okay, it's okay. Don't talk. An ambulance is on its way.'

She struggled to sit up.

'Take it easy.' He pulled her against him and wrapped his arms around her.

'Where's William?

'Gone.'

Chapter Twenty-Nine

He walked out of the drab hospital building, blinked and looked up at the clear, morning sky. It was quiet and warm and only a few people were about. The hospital's cafe had just opened its doors. He could do with a coffee, but decided not to linger, he had work to do.

Jill was wearing a blue hospital gown. She opened her eyes and touched her cheek. Her face felt like it had been rammed against a brick wall. A nurse walked into the room with a clipboard.

'Am I dead?' Jill asked.

'No, you're not dead,' the nurse laughed. 'How are you feeling?'

'Had better days.'

The memory of last night came to her in fragments. The nurse felt Jill's pulse and took her blood pressure.

'I've just started my shift, but one of the nurses on duty last night told me your boyfriend insisted on staying with you last night. He only left when he was satisfied you were going to be okay. Where do you find guys like that?'

Jill didn't know what to make of William and was surprised by the depth of feeling he obviously had for her. She felt guilty. She had treated him badly. She squinted from a slit in her eye and looked out the window across to the multi-decked car park of Royal North Shore Hospital. The day outside was bright; the sky was blue, cloudless. She would rather be any-where, but here.

Five days later and every inch of her body still hurt like hell. Jill returned to the station and all eyes were on her. She was on her way down to the canteen when she passed Rimis in the hall.

'You sure you should be back at work? You know you don't have to be here.'

'Yes, boss, I'm fine,' she lied. Her head ached and her ribs hurt. Luckily her nose wasn't broken. She didn't know what she would do if she sneezed.

'I'm on my way out now, but come and see me later.' He walked on but turned around and called out to her. 'Sure you're okay?'

She smiled but she didn't turn around for him to see it. 'Sure.'

She walked into the canteen and searched her pockets for a couple of coins. She grabbed a can of soft drink from the vending machine and took a seat in the corner.

Luke Rawlings pushed his chair back from the next table, walked over and sat down across from her.

'You sure you should be back at work so soon? You've got a real shiner there.'

Her face was covered in purple, yellow and green bruises. She was aware of how she must look. 'I'm on desk duties until further notice.'

'Want to talk?'

Jill looked at him. 'I can't believe what Kevin did. He's not the first person to have a bad start in life.'

'Maybe it was about the power. After all those years of beatings and being treated the way he was, maybe he wanted to know what it felt like to be in control, to inflict some suffering on someone else.'

'His neighbours must have known what was going on. They would have heard the screams, seen the bruises.'

'Different times. Back then, kids were always getting a hiding.'

'I wonder if Nora ever felt guilty.'

'Who knows, maybe she did in the end.'

Jill didn't know what to do with herself. She felt like she had been run over by a bus. She should have taken extra time off. All she could think of doing right now was going for a swim, tasting the ocean, throwing herself beneath the waves like she used to do with her father. Her phone rang. She looked at the caller ID. 'Sorry, Luke, I have to take this.' It was William. She waited for Luke to walk away before she answered the call.

'How are you?' William asked.

'I'm okay. I'm back at work.'

'Are you sure that's a good idea?'

Why does everyone keep asking me that? 'I'd rather be working than sitting around at home feeling sorry for myself. There's not much you can do for a few bruises and some broken ribs, apart from taking paracetamol.' She tried to laugh.

'Look Jill, I wanted to apologise for not hanging around the other night. With all the commotion, I couldn't handle it. I waited downstairs for the paramedics to arrive and I knew Nick was with you, so I went home.'

Rimis? He must have been the one at her bedside. 'Look William, I know this has all been a bit crazy but —'

'Don't say anything. We both know it would never have worked. What you went through with Kevin, I don't think I could handle knowing every day you went to work you might not come home.'

'It's the job. It's what I do.'

Jill knocked on Rimis's office door and walked in. She was on her way home. Her shift had just finished. Rimis was at the window with his back to her and his hands in his pockets.

He turned around and looked at her. 'Sit down, Brennan. Anyone told you, you look like shit?'

She smiled for the first time in days. 'Thanks, boss. You really know how to make a girl feel good about herself.' She sat down and crossed her arms against her chest.

'How are the ribs? Want to take some more time off?' Rimis sat down in his high-backed office chair.

'No, they're fine, it just hurts now and again if I move the wrong way, or if I laugh.'

'You should take things easy until you're fully recovered.'

'The pain killers are kicking in nicely.'

Rimis studied her for a moment. 'If you harden yourself against it, it'll go away,' he said.

'The pain you mean?'

'No, thinking about Kevin Taggart.'

Jill looked at him. She was surprised and embarrassed by what he could see in her, but she was also surprised by what she saw in him. If she didn't know any better, she would say he was actually worried about her. 'You were right about Kevin. I should have listened to you.'

'If you are going to make a good detective, you have to learn to trust your instincts.'

'How did Kevin slip through the cracks when he was a child? The Blake sisters must have known about the abuse.'

'It might explain why they were so kind to him,' Rimis said.

'Might also explain why he killed them.'

Instead of going home after her shift ended, Jill drove to the Dunworth. She felt guilty she had used Bea's friendship to get a job at the gallery. She tried not to think what would have happened if Kevin Taggart hadn't agreed to exhibit his paintings. Would Freddie and Paloma still be alive? Would Kevin be a free man now, going unpunished for the women he'd murdered?

'What are you doing here?' Bea walked out from the office and wrapped her arms around Jill. After she released her, she stood back and took a good look at her. 'You look like a prize fighter with that black eye.'

A flash of pain shot across her ribs and Jill held her chest. 'I'm fine, just a few bruises.' She shut her eyes to stop the tears. 'If you really want to know, I've had better days.'

'What's happened now?'

Jill bit down on her lip and looked around at the paintings on the wall. It was the opening of the Byron Willis exhibition tomorrow. She swallowed hard and sat down on the timber floor. 'It's all got a bit much. I'm such a mess Bea, I don't think I can go back.'

'What do you mean, you can't go back?' Bea sat down on the floor beside her and held her hands.

'It's no use, Dad was right, I haven't got what it takes.' Jill could feel her eyes welling up again. 'On the way over here, I tried to kid myself it was all part of the job, but what happened with Kevin… It was just horrible. I haven't been sleeping,' she said. 'I've been having these terrible nightmares.'

'What about counselling? Have they offered it to you?'

'Yes, of course, it's policy, but I said no.' Jill wondered if she should tell her about Morrissey's claims that her father was corrupt?

'Are you crazy? After what you've been through? And why the hell are you back at work? You should be on sick leave. What about that boss of yours, Nick Rimis? What does he say about all of this?'

Jill stared at the wall.

'Jill?'

'He's been supportive. I'm on light duties, but —'

'What is it?'

'Maybe I should come to work here at the Gallery, opt out for a quieter life, surround myself with beautiful things and leave the ugly side of life to those who can handle it.'

Bea grabbed hold of her friend's shoulders. 'For as long as I've known you, all you've ever wanted was to become a detective. Are you listening to me? When you first told me you'd resigned and you came to work here, I couldn't believe it.'

'I'm not cut out for the job. Look at me, I'm twenty-eight years old, no family, no friends.'

'What are you talking about no family, no friends. Isn't that what I am? What Harry and Callum are? Remember the day we first met?' Bea asked. 'You were the new girl at Maroubra Public. You told me you were Jillian Eleanor Brennan, you were ten years old, and you were going to be a policeman when you grew up. And I said, you were a girl, so you had to be a policewoman.'

Jill wiped away the tears with the back of her hand.

'I wanted to be an air hostess, remember?' Bea said.

'Yeah, I remember.' Jill laughed.

Bea helped Jill to her feet. 'You'll get through this; you've got through worse. Look, I'm about to close up here. Let's go next door to the Tapas bar and have a drink.'

Jill looked at her friend. 'Sounds good,' she said, 'and Bea —'

'What?' Bea stared at Jill.

'I want you to know, I forgive you for trying to set me up with Scott Carver. But next time you try something like that, I'm going to have to kill you.'

They both laughed and headed out through the front door.

Chapter Thirty

It was early evening, the tide was out. Jill walked down the stairs to the stretch of sand and the first thing she saw were the plastic red roses tied to a steel post. Taped to the wrapping was a photo of Paloma Browne.

It felt good to be away from the Station. She sat down, removed her shoes and dug her feet into the sand. Out on the river, she heard the ruffle and snap of a sail. She looked up and saw a small boat turning its prow into the wind. It sailed past. The wind dropped and there was silence again. She concentrated on her breathing, closed her eyes and tried to conjure up a pleasant memory. She would have liked to have had her father here with her now, to tell him about the Blake murders, about Kevin Taggart, Freddie Winfred, about Morrissey and of what he had been prepared to do, to cover his back. Her father would have been proud to know her art qualifications had given her the confidence to take on the undercover assignment.

'You've chosen a strange place to meet,' Rimis said.

Jill jumped. She hadn't heard him approach. She pushed her shoes aside with her bare feet.

He sat down beside her and looked out at the river. 'You can't imagine anything terrible happening here, can you? It's so peaceful.' Rimis said.

He stretched his legs out in front of him and looked over to where Paloma's body had washed up. A stray dog approached. It lifted his head and barked. Rimis patted it, then pushed it away.

'What worries me is that if Vladu did kill Paloma Browne, he'll probably get away with it,' Jill said.

'Interpol is involved now. If I know anything about small-time criminals like Nicolae Vladu, he'll probably latch onto someone else. He might even get involved with the Romanian Mafia. If he does, he could end up being a liability to them. His days are numbered, no matter which way you look at it.'

Jill pulled her hair out from her ponytail and shook her head. She dug her feet deeper into the sand.

'Find anything out from the solicitor?' He loosened his tie, drew his knees up to his chest.

'Max West wasn't going to tell me, he'd promised my father. I had to practically drag it out of him. Morrissey lied to me. Dad wasn't on the take. The money for my schooling came from some family heirlooms. The jewellery was to have been handed down from mother to daughter, from one generation to the next. Dad sold them to pay off the loan he had for my school fees and to pay for my university fees. I never knew he was ashamed that he couldn't provide for me in the way he wanted to, but Dad was always practical. I'm sure he thought my mother wouldn't have minded.' She picked up a handful of sand and watched it run through her fingers. 'It's my biggest regret, you know.'

'What? That you didn't get to see the family jewels?' Rimis asked.

'No, that I can't remember my mother. You'd think I could remember something, wouldn't you?'

'With memories, it's usually the worst ones that stick around; the pleasant ones drift away,' Rimis said.

Jill looked at him and wondered if he was referring to Kevin Taggart or to himself. 'The solicitor couldn't explain the fifty-thousand dollars. It was a cash deposit, banked at the Commonwealth Bank in George Street in the city.'

'I can help you there,' Rimis said. 'Morrissey confessed to everything. He banked the money into Mickey's account. It was a form of insurance, in case Mickey was ever tempted to report him. I don't know whether Mickey knew anything about the theft, but Col thought he did. The only problem was, once the money was in his account, Morrissey couldn't get his hands on it again. He could never have predicted Mickey would be shot two days after he'd banked the money.

'Funny about people, isn't it? You think you know them, but you don't really. I would never have thought Morrissey capable of half the things he's admitted to.'

'So why did he even bother to tell me about what he was up to?'

'You were a threat to him. You were getting too close to Chisca and he was worried he might let you in on a few secrets.'

They sat together in silence for the next five minutes.

'You and I, we're alike, you know,' she said.

'What do you mean?'

'We're both loners.'

'So, you heard my wife left me?'

'Not that. Not even because I know you live on your own. I think it's in your nature. I think that's why the job suits us both.'

It was Rimis who broke the silence. 'There's a pub down the road. Want to get something to eat?'

The next morning, Jill walked into the station. Waiting to hear the results of the Bull Ring interview was killing her, but at least life was getting back to normal. Though she wasn't sure what normal was anymore. Her black eye was fading and her ribs weren't hurting as much thanks to the painkillers she was taking.

When she overtook Luke Rawlings on the stairs, he looked at her and winked. Jenny Choi rushed past her with files under her arm in the corridor and grinned at her on her way out to a call. It seemed everyone, including the duty sergeant, was in a good mood this morning. When she passed Rimis's office, the door was open and he called out to her.

'Brennan, I've got a letter here for you. But maybe it's not for you.'

She looked at him, puzzled. Rimis got to his feet and walked out from his office. He waved the envelope in front of her.

'It's addressed to Plain Clothes Constable Brennan.'

'What did you say?' Her eyes widened and her face broke into a large smile.

'And, you've been fast tracked. You start the detective's education programme next month.'

Jill hugged him, kissed him on the cheek. Rimis blushed.

'I can't believe it, I can't believe it,' she said. She walked away, almost running, but she wasn't sure where she was going. Halfway down the corridor, she remembered the letter and ran back to him and grabbed it from his hand.

'You'll make a great detective one day, Brennan. You've got the nose for it, you know what I mean?'

Jill smiled. She knew exactly what Nick Rimis meant.

Acknowledgements.

Among the many people I would like to thank for their assistance in writing and producing this book, I would like to make special mention of Toni Eatts and Eva Molinar for their encouragement and input. Thank you also to those who read and commented on the later drafts of *Killing Sunday* and to Katherine Tierney who advised me on the process involved in becoming a detective in the New South Wales Police Service. Also thank you to Annie Werner for supplying information on tattoos.

Thank you Amanda Hampson, Laurel Cohn, Siboney Duff, and PD Martin for your suggestions and editorial services.

Most of all, I would like to thank all my friends and family for their ongoing emotional support.